To Live Again

By Lauralee Bliss

Writers Exchange E-Publishing

http://www.writers-exchange.com

To Live Again

Copyright 2001, 2013, 2015, 2018, 2022 Lauralee Bliss

Writers Exchange E-Publishing

PO Box 372

ATHERTON QLD 4883

Cover Art by: Sandy Cummins and GermanCreative

Published by Writers Exchange E-Publishing

http://www.writers-exchange.com

Weeping may endure for the night, but joy cometh in the morning.

Psalm 30:5 KJV

Chapter 1

"We're going to be late!" Janice Dawson moaned. Her eyes darted to the golden anniversary clock sitting on the fireplace mantel. "Mary, put on your shoes. Lisa, come here and let Mommy tie on your hair ribbons."

Five-year-old Lisa shuffled into the living room, her tiny fist clutching the piece of pink ribbon that matched the ruffles on her Sunday dress. Limping behind her in stocking feet came eight-year-old Mary. She held one shoe in her hand with confusion written in her dark brown eyes.

"I don't know where my other shoe is, Mommy," Mary complained.

Janice picked up the ribbon from Lisa's outstretched hand and looped it around the ponytail behind her head. She stole another glance at the clock ticking down to their departure time. "Look under your bed or in the coat closet. Really girls, I must be there on time today. Last week I was late and I can't do this two weeks in a row."

"Where's Daddy?" Lisa inquired. She reached up her hand to tug on the ponytail Janice fashioned. Brown hair fell in soft tendrils around her face. The ribbon came to a rest at her feet.

"Oh Lisa, now look what you did!" With a swipe of her hand, Janice yanked off the hair band. The tiny girl shrieked, accompanied by tears that squirted out of her hazel eyes and rolled down her cheeks. "Oh honey, I'm so sorry," Janice murmured, scooping the distraught child into her arms. "When Mommy gets woken up in the middle of the night and can't go back to sleep, she ends up a mean ol' grouch. I know I shouldn't take it out on you."

Lisa giggled, even as her fist wiped away the tears. "Did Daddy go help with the babies again, Mommy?"

Janice nodded, once more fixing Lisa's hair by twisting the soft strands in her fingers and slipping on a hair band. "Yes. Daddy got a call in the middle of the night. Mrs. Clark is ready to have her baby."

"So Daddy is at the hospital?" Mary inquired. She tugged on the other patent leather shoe found beneath the couch, then waited patiently for Janice to fasten it to her foot.

"Yes. I haven't heard anything, so I guess he's still there." Janice sighed, swiping back a lock of wavy brown hair that fell across her forehead before her fingers fumbled to fasten the buckle on Mary's shoe.

"Daddy sure helps bring a lot of babies," Mary remarked.

"That's his job, honey. He's a family doctor, you know, and that's what doctors do." She stood to her feet and picked up her purse and Bible from the counter. "All right, I think we're finally ready."

Both girls skipped ahead of Janice who closed the solid oak door behind them with a thump. Bright sunshine greeted her on this pleasant spring day. She wished Len was here to accompany the family to church, but the flight of expectant mothers racing to the hospital in the middle of the night was a fact of life for a family practitioner. Despite Len's success with his medical practice and her happy home life, Janice felt herself on edge these days. She could not settle a terrible sense of foreboding welling up within her. Every night she thanked God in her prayers for the love of her husband, the stylish house they owned, the lovely gardens she managed with care, and her healthy daughters that never ceased to amuse her with their childish antics. Yet she worried that one day her beautiful life might come to an end. Len laughed when she confessed her fear the other night after the girls were tucked in bed.

"This isn't something to laugh about, Len," she told him, wiggling her way out of his arms and climbing to her feet. She paced the carpeted floor of their master suite in agitation. "We've enjoyed so many blessings...I'm afraid I'm due for a healthy dose of tribulation any day now."

"Jan, if you allow your Christianity to bring forth fear and not faith, what good is it? God wants you to trust Him and not your circumstances." Len rose from the bed at that point. His six-foot frame towered over her five-foot-five in a picture of strength and security. His dark eyes that she found so appealing stared lovingly into her face, tracing every defining line of her narrow cheeks, sloped nose, and green eyes that he said reminded him of the dazzling Emerald City in the *Wizard of Oz*.

"I know I should be thankful," she murmured, enjoying the feel of his arms curled around her. "You have such a wonderful job with this family practice, and we have two sweet girls...."

"...and I have a beautiful and talented wife," he finished, supplementing his statement with a kiss that for several moments diverted her thoughtful contemplation.

Janice dwelt on the kiss and the delightful intimacy shared afterwards until Mary's girlish voice piped up.

"Mommy, aren't we going to church?"

Janice awoke from her dream to realize she had not yet started the engine. "There goes my mind," she murmured, shaking her head and turning the key in the ignition. "I'm thinking of Len when I'm supposed to be driving us to our Sunday school class." She proceeded down the tree-lined drive of the affluent neighborhood where they had purchased a home only a year ago. She missed Len on the weekends when he had to work. During the week, she was involved with a hum of daily activities that included home schooling her girls in the morning and running a cake decorating business in the afternoon. Janice was grateful for the fine home, complete with a large gourmet kitchen where she could fashion her cakes. The girls loved to watch her create a funny Big Bird or a sweet ballerina out of the cakes she baked in the oven. Creating and decorating cakes in her spare time allowed Janice the opportunity to put her skills to use while keeping the girls at home with her. Most of all, she was happy that Len supported her work - even helping her finance the bakeware and the purchase of a convection oven.

"He's so sweet to me," Janice murmured, steering the car into the parking lot of the neighborhood church. "Oh, how I miss him." An idea suddenly sparked in her mind. Perhaps after the service, she could surprise Len with Sunday dinner at the hospital. She glowed at the thought of his reaction to the gesture - his dark eyes lighting up and a smile creasing his face, displaying the even white teeth in contrast to his tan complexion. "I can buy a box of chicken from the market, along with some side dishes," she mused, "and of course we'll need dinner rolls, paper plates, perhaps a gallon of sweetened iced tea..."

"Hi Lisa! Hi Mary!" A cheery voice greeted the family when they entered the foyer of the church.

"Aunt Katy!" the girls cried together. They raced into the arms of a tall woman with chestnut brown hair and a large smile, stylishly dressed in a two piece suit.

Janice was still thinking about the surprise dinner for Len when she felt a tap on her shoulder. She whirled in a start to find a set of familiar dark brown eyes peering steadily into her own.

"Len!"

Laughter filled her ears. "Ah ha, so he left you alone again, did he?"

Janice turned her head away to avoid him seeing the crimson flush that tainted her cheeks. "I'm so sorry, Paul. I don't know why I do that to you all the time."

"Not all the time," he corrected good-naturedly. "Just when you miss my brother. You're forgiven."

"So is Len at the hospital again?" Katy inquired, her arms cradling her two little nieces.

Janice nodded while trying to regain her composure. "Yes. We got a call around two in the morning. One of his patients, Mrs. Clark, went into early labor. He knew this would be a difficult delivery."

"You poor thing." Katy stared over at Paul. "I bet you didn't sleep a wink the rest of the night."

Janice eyed her in amazement. "How did you know?"

"Because we know how much you two love each other. It's hard to sleep without your honey by your side to kiss you good night."

"Mommy and Daddy kiss a lot," Lisa remarked.

"That means they love each other," Mary added.

"That's right," agreed their Uncle Paul who suddenly grabbed Katy in an affectionate hold. "So what does this mean, girls?" He proceeded to plant a firm kiss on her rosy lips.

Katy pushed him away. "Really Paul, and in church, too!"

"I was greeting you with a holy kiss," he said innocently, but with a mischievous grin.

"Enough of the holy kisses. Our nieces are late for their Sunday school class."

"I guess Pat, Dan, and Karen are already in their classes?" Janice remarked, glancing around for the three children belonging to Paul and Katherine Dawson.

"Yes, so you'd better go on to your classes," Katy instructed the two girls, patting their heads affectionately. She added, "And why don't we mosey on in to ours?"

Janice was grateful on this lonely Sunday for the companionship of Len's older brother Paul and his wife Katherine or Katy, as she was known. Janice walked behind the couple who held hands as they entered the church sanctuary, thinking of the family resemblance between Paul and Len. Despite the five years difference in their ages, both men possessed the dark brown eyes and tawny complexion of the Dawson line. Paul's hair already showed telltale signs of aging with gray streaks running through his head of black hair. Len maintained his youthful appearance with hardly a gray hair to be found. Just the other day, Janice teased Len at finding a solitary gray hair among the jet-black strands on his head. "Soon you'll look just like Paul," she joked.

"I certainly hope not."

Janice frowned at the sharp retort. Despite their appearance, both brothers were staunchly different, waging a silent war from the past that kept them apart for most of their adult years. When Janice tried to broach Len on the subject, he only swatted away her concerns and steered the conversation around to her cake decorating business.

Janice knew better than to allow the subject to slip, but once he engaged her in conversation about her favorite pastime--cake decorating, she couldn't help herself. Immediately she launched into her ideas for her first wedding cake, explaining in detail the lacy design in the frosting, accompanied by wedding bells on the top tier. The job itself proved tedious, but the results were stunning. Janice delivered the cake with confidence to the reception hall and found the bride overwhelmed by the presentation. The next day, a photographer and journalist arrived at the house, eager to run a story about her in-home cake decorating business in the lifestyle section of the newspaper.

"You're famous!" Len exclaimed to Janice, giving her a hug as they scanned the article that followed.

Janice only wondered when all this would come to a screeching halt. She flipped through her Bible, searching absentmindedly for the Gospel of Matthew, which the congregation had been studying the last several weeks. She never noticed Katy give her a sideways glance before whispering to Paul. He nodded and rose. Janice jerked her head around and jumped when she found him sitting down beside her.

"Since you miss Len so much, Katy thought I could help out," Paul whispered with a twinkle in his eye.

"Don't be silly, Paul. I know I mistake you for Len all the time, but you really don't look that much alike. You have too much gray hair, for one thing."

He chuckled. "Then just pretend I'm Len. That way you can concentrate on the pastor, knowing your husband is right here by your side. Here, you can look at my phone with me, I have it right here."

Janice shook her head, forcing a smile at his suggestion. "Nice try Paul, but you will never be Len. Your personalities are like night and day."

Paul snapped his fingers in mock rejection to the annoyance of two elderly ladies sitting in the pew directly in front of them. One lady turned and gave them both an icy glare.

"You're getting us in trouble with the Addington sisters!" Janice whispered furiously. "Go back and sit with Katy where you belong."

He raised his hands in defeat. "All right, I tried. But from now on, keep your mind on what's going on in the pulpit."

"Thanks, I will," Janice promised, accompanied by a sheepish grin. Paul winked and returned to his rightful place beside Katy. For the remainder of the Bible class and throughout the service that followed, Janice concentrated on the words spoken by the pastor and the songs of praise that filled her heart. Afterward she was greeted by many of the congregation who commented on Len's absence from the service. Janice maintained her composure during the cumbersome task of informing everyone of Len's late night duty at the hospital. When she managed to tear herself and the girls away, she hurried outside to the car. The voice of a young boy halted her steps.

"Aunt Jan!" he cried, waving his hand. Janice turned to see her ten-year-old nephew, Daniel, running to catch up. "Hey, Dad and Mom want to know if you can come over for lunch today."

Janice watched Paul and Katy in the background with their two other children by their side - eleven-year-old Patrick who was an image of Len in his younger days, and eight-year-old Karen, the same age as Mary. "I can't today, Dan. Tell your mom and dad I plan on surprising Uncle Len with lunch at the hospital."

"Okay," he acknowledged, rushing off to deliver the news.

Janice ushered the girls to the car and fastened their seat belts securely.

"So we're gonna see Daddy at work?" Lisa wondered, staring down at the picture of Jesus in her hands, colored in with crayons during her Sunday school class.

"I think it would be a nice surprise. I'll call the hospital, though, just to make sure he's not in the middle of a delivery." Janice fumbled in her purse for the cell phone. Her fingers trembled while punching in the number for the hospital.

"I'm sorry, but Dr. Dawson is unable to speak with you right now," a haughty voice informed her.

"Is he involved with a delivery?"

"Not at this time."

"This is Dr. Dawson's wife and I would like to speak with him." Janice tried to steady her voice, all the while wondering who was the new nurse on duty. Most of the OB staff at the University Hospital recognized her voice and were prompt in bringing Len to the phone unless he was involved with a delivery.

Again the nurse snapped, "I'm sorry, but he can't come to the phone. I suggest you call his answering service and leave a message. Thank you."

A dial tone met her startled ears. Janice stared at the cell phone in dismay before flinging it into her purse. "We'll see about that!" she huffed.

"What's the matter, Mommy?" asked Mary.

Janice smiled shakily in an effort to settle the concerned expressions filtering across the faces of her daughters. "Oh, it's nothing, honey. I guess Daddy's pretty busy at the hospital. I'm wondering now whether we should bring him lunch."

"I want to see the babies," Lisa protested.

"Yeah Mommy, let's go see the babies," Mary chimed in. "That way you'll know if Daddy's busy or not."

"That's a good idea," Janice admitted, driving out onto the highway. "We'll stop at the market and grab a few items for lunch. Maybe we can steal Daddy away for a quick bite to eat."

Both girls giggled at the idea of stealing their daddy with a delightful noise that warmed Janice's heart. The oldest daughter, Mary, displayed a carefree personality in contrast with her younger sister, Lisa, who proved studious and quiet. Janice often wondered what she would do without the companionship of her two girls during the lonely times when Len was away. She cherished the ability to keep her girls at home with her during the day. Many of her friends objected to her decision to school the girls at home. They warned her that she would grow weary of them and feel unsatisfied as a mere keeper of the home. Yet Janice did not feel anything but satisfaction with the way she was bringing up her girls, along with having her cake decorating business on the side. She enjoyed the idea of teaching her girls reading, writing, and arithmetic in conjunction with her beliefs in the Bible. Hearing the childish whispers in the backseat as Mary read to Lisa out of one of her books, Janice felt proud to have taught them.

Janice steered the car into the hospital parking garage after picking up lunch at a nearby market. The mouth-watering aroma of chicken filled the car. Everywhere she looked, people were scurrying into the stunning brick and white complex of the University Hospital, holding flower arrangements or other gifts for the sick. Janice picked up the food bags, and with her girls in tow, walked across the causeway above the busy thoroughfare below. Once inside the elevator, she allowed the girls to push the button for the eighth floor that housed the obstetrics unit. When the steel doors parted, the shrill of newborn babies in their bassinets met their ears. The girls' childish voices begged Janice to see the tiny infants.

"We'll go right after we find your father," Janice whispered. She came to the nurses' station and breathed a sigh of relief at finding the friendly face of Cathy McPherson, one of the staff nurses who often assisted Len in delivery. "Hi Cathy," she greeted the young woman manning a seat before a computer screen with a pen light in her fingers.

Instead of her usual perky smile and friendly greeting, the woman looked up at her in surprise. "Why Janice, didn't they tell you downstairs?"

"Tell me what?"

"Dr. Dawson...I mean your husband...he's....he's in the emergency room. He suffered an attack a short time go and....."

"No!" Janice cried, leaving the lunch bags at the nurse's station and rushing for the nearest elevator, dragging her girls behind. *No!* Her mind screamed in panic. *Not Len, please God!*

Chapter 2

Janice arrived breathless to the emergency room to find her beloved husband dressing in his clothes while fighting with the attending ER physician who insisted he have a battery of tests to determine the cause of his pain. "It's acute cholecystitis, Harry," Leonard Dawson argued, pushing buttons through the buttonholes to his shirt when Janice rushed into his arms.

"Oh Len, I was so worried!"

"There's nothing to worry about," he told her soothingly. "I'm fine. I just had a little spell after the delivery was over. It's nothing."

"He refuses to have us perform an abdominal ultrasound," the emergency room doctor stated, obviously vexed over Len's decision. "I tell you, doctors are the most obstinate beings. They think they're omniscient or something."

"Len, maybe you should have them...," Janice began.

"It isn't necessary," he interrupted. "I keep telling this guy it's my gallbladder. It runs in the family. Paul had his out a few years ago, you remember that, Jan. Dad had the same surgery back when he was my age. All the Dawson men suffer with it. It's an inherited trait. One of these days I'm gonna have an internist look at it, but now's not the time. There's too much going on." He jammed his feet into his winged-tip shoes, then turned toward his daughters who stared at him with their large eyes. "Daddy's fine," he assured them before sweeping the pair into his arms. "How about a kiss?"

"We brought you lunch, Daddy," Mary announced.

"Fried chicken!" added Lisa.

"I wish I could eat it, but I'm afraid fried chicken is the last thing I want to give a bad gallbladder. Clogs everything up inside. But I'll watch you eat it for me if that's okay with you."

"Actually we left the lunch at the nurse's station after Cathy told me you were down here in Emergency," Janice remarked.

Len chuckled. "I'm sure the nurses will enjoy the free food. The food around here is enough to give anyone acute cholecystitis, right Harry?"

"I'm not saying anything more, Len, or I'm liable to blow my stack," the doctor retorted before striding off to examine another patient hidden behind a curtain on the opposite side of the room.

"I need to check on my patient in OB, then we can go home."

"Did everything go all right with the mother?" Janice inquired as they headed for the elevator.

"It was a close one but she finally delivered. I was afraid she might require an emergency cesarean the way her labor was progressing."

"You must be exhausted," Janice crooned, rubbing the back of his neck.

"I am pretty tired," he admitted. He winced in pain as his fingers probed the area of tenderness just below his right rib cage.

Janice couldn't help but notice his discomfort that set off her own painful worries. "Are you sure you shouldn't have that checked out, Len? What if it's something serious?"

"It isn't, Jan, so please stop worrying about it. Go ahead and wait for me by the main entrance and I'll be down in a jiffy." He planted a kiss on her cheek.

"All right." Janice watched him enter the elevator and the doors close over a crooked smile on his face before he disappeared to the obstetrics unit. She turned with a sigh and entered the waiting room to ponder the strange occurrence down in emergency while Mary and Lisa went to investigate the large tank of tropical fish displayed in the corner. Len never complained of pain as far as she could recollect. He did appear thinner these days. His appetite had slacked off in the last several weeks, which she attributed to a busy schedule that did not allow him time for proper meals. The combination of these factors gave her an uneasy feeling, as if something lurked within him, waiting to rear its ugly head when she least expected it.

Her foot tapped the thick carpet until she heard his familiar voice calling for her. Len's appearance inside the waiting room startled her. His pinched face and dark circles below his eyes renewed her fears. Something was definitely wrong. "Are you sure you're all right, honey?"

"Just fine," he said, managing a tight smile. "Pain's nearly gone. It's typical with this kind of thing, Jan, especially if you've passed a gallstone which is probably what happened."

"You have stones inside you, Daddy?" Mary asked, slipping her hand into his.

Len chuckled. "I forgot that we have two inquisitive girls." He turned to address his eldest daughter who stared up at him with a set of large brown eyes like her father. "Not really, Mary. It's not the kind of stone you're thinking of, although a gallstone can be shaped like a tiny pebble you find out in the road. Sometimes inside your tummy you get these little pebbles that form from the foods we eat. They get stuck inside the tubes and cause pain."

Mary nodded, satisfied by the simple explanation.

"So is that what your father and Paul both had?" Janice wondered as they crossed over the causeway toward their respective cars nestled within the parking garage.

"Exactly. Nothing to worry about. Race you home."

"Maybe I should drive you home instead..." she began.

A frown tugged down the corners of his mouth. "Now Jan, don't start babying me. I'm fine. I wouldn't attempt to drive if I wasn't. You all mean too much to me."

"All right," she conceded, watching him saunter off to his car. She opened the rear door for her girls, wishing she felt the same confidence as Len did concerning his condition. Shivers raced up her spine at the mere idea of something medically wrong with him. Perhaps she should call Paul and ask for his feedback concerning this gallbladder disease inflicting the family. She only prayed that God would give her the strength and the wisdom to navigate her through whatever lie ahead.

When they arrived home, Len immediately went into the master bedroom to recover from his exhausting night. Janice entertained the girls with a story while they sat together cozily on the couch. Outside the window on an azalea bush, a bird chirped a merry song. Lisa jumped to her feet and raced over to observe the bird in the midst of his musical serenade. Flowers stood poised to bloom from the buds scattered along the branches. Janice and Mary joined in the observation of the bird before he flew off to unite with his feathery companions on an electrical wire spanning the street.

"What kind of bird was that, Mommy?" Mary wondered, resting her head against Janice's shoulder.

Janice ran her fingers through the soft brown strands of her daughter's hair. "I'm not sure, honey. We should check out a bird book from the library and start looking up the birds around here. Now that it's spring, the birds have returned to build their nests."

"Where did they go?" Mary wondered.

"Once winter comes, they fly down south where it's nice and warm. Birds don't like the cold weather, you see. They go to some of the marshlands way down in Florida or even to the country of Mexico. When the warm weather returns, they fly back here to have their babies."

"So the birds are gonna have babies?" Lisa asked, joining Mary by occupying the other shoulder.

Janice felt the heavy warmth of her daughters' heads resting on each shoulder pad to her flowered top; each of them drawing strength and wisdom from the reservoirs of knowledge she had acquired over the years. "Yes, but first they must build their nests. In fact," she pointed to an oak tree on the front lawn, "you can see the beginnings of a nest way up there in the branches. See all those twigs poking out?"

Mary lifted her head and scrunched her eyes to gain a better view. "Yeah, sort of."

"That's a bird's nest. After the birds build their nests, the mother bird has her babies. The mother bird lays her eggs, then sits on them for a long time until the babies hatch."

"Oh, I wish I could pet the babies birds," Lisa purred. "I bet they're cute!"

"It's not a good idea to touch a mother bird's babies," Janice warned. "Birds don't like our smell on their babies. I've even heard of mother birds killing their babies if they have a strange smell on them."

Both girls sat straight up and stared at their mother with tearful eyes. When Janice saw the sorrowful girls before her, she regretted her choice of words. "I'm sorry," she apologized, giving them a squeeze. "I didn't mean to upset you, but now you know why we mustn't go near a bird's nest."

"We won't," both girls promised before Janice rose to fetch them fruit juice pops from the freezer. Once she settled them at the table with their frozen treats, she tiptoed up the stairs and down the hall, peering inside the master bedroom to check on Len. The quilt was rumpled and the pillow depressed where his stout form once lay. She came into the bathroom to see him hunched over the sink; the pain sending ripples running across his lean face.

"Len, are you all right?" Janice rubbed his back, murmuring a prayer for him under her breath.

"Oh sure. Just woke up with a slight twinge." He straightened to stare at his appearance in the mirror while combing his fingers through his head of black hair. "Even though my age says I'm young, I don't feel young."

"It's all those long nights you're putting in. Isn't there some way that Mike can be on call during the night until you're feeling better?" Mike Free was Len's devoted partner in the family practice - a newly licensed medical doctor and a Christian who took his position seriously. Janice was glad when Len signed him on after the other two practitioners he had worked with mysteriously departed the office in search of other employment. At first Janice was horrified when Len came home one day to announce he was alone in the practice. "But what happened?" she pressed. He only shrugged his shoulders and said there were differences in their work ethics. Finally he revealed that the two practitioners were counseling unmarried pregnant women to obtain abortions and save their livelihoods - a practice totally against Len's belief in the sanctity of human life. When Len confronted the fellow doctors on the issue, a huge debate ensued. The practitioners promptly left to set up their own clinic on the opposite side of town, leaving Len to run the office on his own. The bills began to mount. Several nurses on staff had to be dismissed. A year later, he had the fortunate opportunity of meeting young Michael Free who held to a similar philosophy of doctoring and agreed to join the practice.

"I might put him on call for night duty next week," Len decided as he examined the dark circles under his eyes from the lack of sleep. He rearranged his trousers, tucked in his polo shirt, and cinched the belt another notch.

"You're losing weight, too," Janice observed in dismay. "Really Len, can I fix you something to eat? You're not eating enough, you know. Soon you'll be so skinny that..."

"Janice, I'm hearing Lucinda again." He shuffled out of the room to find Mary and Lisa.

Janice frowned at the remark. Her mother, Lucinda Harris, was a domineering woman who complained continually. "It's easy to see why her marriage never worked," Len would remark in reference to Janice's parents who divorced when she was a teenager. Janice rarely dwelt on that time of emotional upheaval in her life. Her father had never been happy with the constant bickering of her mother, yet Janice knew it was wrong of him to seek consolation in the arms of another woman. The day her parents announced their divorce was one of the saddest days in Janice's life. Her father promptly married the woman he had the affair with, and moved to a remote location on the West Coast. She rarely saw him.

Since that time, Lucinda Harris had been the controlling factor in Janice's life, including her initial relationship with Len. When she and Len first met, Lucinda insisted on interviewing him to see if he was, as she put it, "of appropriate caliber for marriage to my only daughter." Len went along with the inquisition out of his love for her, but Janice couldn't help but be embarrassed by it all. After many prayerful nights, Lucinda finally accepted Len. Now whenever Janice nagged Len about something, he would toss out the line that reminded them of the personality trait inherent in her mother.

Janice inhaled a deep breath, determined not to allow her anxiety over his medical condition to dictate her actions. After all, wasn't Len a medical doctor who knew all about the human body? Surely he would know what to do and when to do it. She managed to put a smile on her face before walking into the living room to see Len engaging their daughters in a game of

Candyland. He sat with the little girls companionably on the soft carpet, dividing the huge stack of colored cards into two piles.

"Would you like to play?" he asked Janice with a wink.

"Sure I'll play. Which color is left?"

"You can be the blue man," Lisa said, placing her piece on the board.

"You aren't blue now, are you, Jan?" Len asked, seemingly studying the expression of optimism she had tried to paint on her worried face.

"I'm trying not to be," she said, avoiding his look. They took turns picking up the cards containing colored rectangles and moving their men to the appropriate colored block on the board. Whenever a certain piece of candy was drawn that either advanced the colored men or sent them back, groans or cheers were offered. Janice managed to place her man halfway up the board when she chose the ill-fated plum card, sending her blue man back to the beginning.

"Poor Mommy," said Lisa in sympathy, accompanied by a pat on the arm.

Mary pulled out the snowflake card that sent her yellow man soaring to the top of the game board near the Candyland castle.

"Mary's gonna win!" Janice noted with a smile.

"No, she's not," Lisa countered.

Len remained stranded on a blue rectangle with a black dot, waiting to pick up a blue card from the pile so he might continue on with his journey. At last Mary entered the Candyland castle with her final draw of a card.

"I won, I won!" she laughed with glee.

"Winning isn't everything," Len told Lisa when she began to cry. He scooped the distraught girl into his arms and gave her a hug.

"I wanna play again!" Mary announced.

The family played two more rounds of the game before Janice rose to stretch her cramped extremities and suggested they all go for a walk around the block. The girls eagerly pounced on the idea and grabbed for their sneakers. While Janice slipped on her shoes, she again noticed the tightly pressed lips and lines of tension streaking across Len's face.

"Is it another attack?" she asked quietly.

He only waved it away and announced to the girls, "Okay, last one to the mailbox has to do the dishes tonight!"

Everyone jumped to their feet and giggled as they tore off down the blacktop with hands straining for the aluminum mailbox on its cedar support erected at the base of the driveway. Len purposely slowed his pace, allowing Mary to reach the box first where she announced her superiority over her little sister. Len comforted Lisa by taking up her tiny hand in his. Together they strolled down the sidewalk. He pointed out a neighbor's collection of tulips or a flowering dogwood tree nearing its peak bloom. The crisp air and fluffy clouds drifting lazily across the indigo sky made for a pleasant afternoon. The family began sharing ideas of where they wanted to go on their summer trip when Len took his vacation time during the last two weeks of July. Mary and Lisa both voiced votes for the beach. Janice only remained thoughtful as she shuffled along the sidewalk, taking in the beauty of the bright spring day around her.

"And where does Mommy want to go?" Len asked.

"Wherever you are," she whispered in his ear, sending a grin spreading across his face. Her hand slipped around his firm biceps, feeling the ripple of muscle beneath her fingertips. The sensation reminded her of his muscular physique when they first met. Len regularly lifted weights nine years ago while in the midst of completing his residency at the University Hospital. At that time, both of them attended the same church, but rarely interacted. When a few adventuresome types within the congregation gathered together for an outing in the mountains, Janice decided to tag along. Len also went on the trip. They struck up a conversation and soon began seeing each other at numerous church functions. After several outings, it became quite clear to Janice that Len was no ordinary man. She eagerly anticipated any opportunity to spend time with him while he put in long hours completing his medical residency to become a full-fledged medical doctor. When she met Len's older brother, Paul, who was already married to Katy and had rambunctious toddlers underfoot, the couple was eager to see them married.

Janice never forgot the night of his proposal. At a quaint German restaurant under a drippy candle, Len's dark eyes appeared like bright pinpoints reflecting the candle's flame when he presented her with the engagement ring. Their marriage was indeed a dream come true. Since that day, Janice lived out her life fulfilled in every way. Now as they circled the block for the return trip home, she only hoped she had the strength to cope with this strange malady that seemed to drain away his youthful vitality. Steadfast prayer and a little nurturing on her part would surely drive out the strange disease inflicting him.

"I hardly slept a wink after the hospital called you last night," Janice confessed that evening in their bedroom, running a brush through her shoulder length brown hair that curled naturally at the ends. She yawned and tossed the brush on the nightstand. "Did you call the hospital about your patient?"

"So far so good," Len acknowledged with equal weariness. "Both Mrs. Clark and the baby are doing fine. But tomorrow's another day and probably a busy one."

"Len, are you still having any more of those pains?" Janice wondered.

"I feel fine," he assured her, accompanied by a yawn. "Don't worry, Jan. If it will make you feel better, I'll call a doctor and get myself checked out."

"Thanks, honey." Janice leaned over to plant a kiss on his cheek, then deposited another one on his lips. When she drew back, he had already fallen asleep, exhausted by the unending spiral of events during the last twenty-four hours. Janice gently brushed back a lock of dark hair falling over his forehead and ran her finger across one prickly cheek. She marveled at the deep earthy skin color of the Dawson family line, giving Len the color of a perpetual tan year round. Len claimed the color had to do with some kind of Indian blood in their family. His older brother Paul often joked that his Indian ancestry was to blame for his wild nature. Paul's wife Katy would shake her head and scold him for his rashness. Len, however, lacked such wildness about him. He was sincere, studious, and devoted to his family and his patients. Janice snuggled next to Len's quiet form, thanking God that He gave her a man like him.

Chapter 3

"Hey, this isn't fair! I'm outnumbered three to one!"

Paul Dawson stared at the children arrayed before him, breathing hard after attempting to chase down his eldest son, Patrick, who held onto the football for dear life. He paused, wiped the sweat from his brow, and inhaled several more deep breaths to settle the pounding of his heart inside his chest. Already his Rugby shirt was saturated with perspiration and clung to his skin like a limp towel.

"C'mon Dad!" Pat and Dan called to him. Even little Karen waved a hand at him, urging him to try and tag them.

"All right, here it goes." He counted to three silently to himself, took a runner's stance, then chased after the boys who made a mad dash for the end zone plotted out by stones. He reached the goal line as Pat yelled, "Touchdown!", then collapsed into a mound of soft grass. His chest heaved as he inhaled deep breaths of crisp air. "All right, you guys win. I'm bushed. I need a breather."

The boys only took advantage of Paul's vulnerability to wrestle. One pinned an arm to the ground while another grabbed for his muscular thigh.

"Hey, what is this? Attack of the killer kids?"

"C'mon Dad," they urged. Even Karen joined in the fun, grabbing hold of Paul's upper arm and yanking at it while urging him to defend himself against the onslaught.

"Look you kids, I'm tuckered out! I had to stand all day in front of a bunch of obnoxious high school students who would rather be texting their friends than listen to me teach English. My legs've had it!"

Finally the kids piled off and sat in the grass, grinning at their exhausted father. "I wish I was old enough to be in your school, Dad," Pat remarked.

"Be glad we have the money to send you to that good Christian school down the road, mister. It's a fine institution."

"Mary's mommy teaches her at home," Karen remarked.

"Your mommy has to work, Karen, to support all this fine education you're receiving. My teacher's salary just doesn't cut it." He sat up slowly, brushing back locks of his salt and pepper colored hair. "Who wants to go for ice cream?"

"Me! Me!" shouted the kids who immediately scrambled to their feet and headed toward the minivan.

Paul took one sniff of his clothes and decided if he did not change, the management of the Dairy Queen down the road would never allow him to set one foot inside the establishment. He ventured into the modest ranch house to be greeted by the strong odor of onions and garlic permeating the air.

"Homemade spaghetti sauce?" he inquired of his wife Katy as she stirred the thick concoction around in a huge iron kettle. He kissed her earlobe. The sweet scent of gardenia she always wore drifted to his nostrils and kindled his passion. He now began nibbling the curved portion of her regal neck that reminded him of royalty. The loving response elicited a girlish giggle.

Katy's hand swatted him away. "Stop, that tickles!"

"Ah ha, so I have found your weakness!" He proceeded to kiss the other ear, whispering in a diabolical voice, "Now you will give me all that I ask for and more or I will torment you!"

"I'm warning you, I'm deadly with a spoon dipped in hot sauce." She whirled around to stare at his sweaty form and the grass clinging to his shirt. "But I think right now the odor of garlic would be a blessed relief."

He laughed. "All right, I can take the hint. I'm changing anyway. I promised to take the kids out to Dairy Queen after they creamed me in touch football."

"Oh Paul, I don't want them spoiling their dinner!"

"Dinner's not for another couple of hours," he said, leaning forward to kiss her ear once more.

"Hey!" she exclaimed, raising the spoon in a threatening gesture.

"Okay, I'm leaving." He whistled while heading to the back bedroom of the modest ranch house where he withdrew another pair of jeans and a clean shirt from the dresser drawer. The bedroom bloomed with Katy's feminine touches. He wondered at the manliness of sleeping under a rose print quilt with matching curtains adorning the windows. She also insisted on a rose-colored shower curtain and matching window treatment in the master bath. Paul sighed and threw his dirty clothes on the floor, then thought better of his action and deposited the clothes into the wicker hamper kept in the corner. Katy constantly harped on his untidiness. Often she would praise the blessings of having a daughter to teach domestic chores after running around tidying up behind her boys. She spoke of the great fortune of his brother, Len, and wife, Janice, at having two girls to rear. "There's no dirty underwear lying in the middle of the hallway, or wet towels thrown on the floor, or blue and green splotches of toothpaste smeared all over the counter."

While Paul loved his little girl, he felt himself fortunate to also have two robust boys. A kid at heart, he enjoyed all sports. This season he planned to be an assistant coach of Dan's baseball team. After observing the team from the sidelines last season and watching in disgust when the boys played in a disjointed manner rather than as a team, Paul pledged to become involved. He was a natural with the young students, even at school. Often he heard the remarks of parents who boasted that his ninth grade English class was their child's favorite. Paul was not sure why he was so successful in his teaching career. Perhaps he could attribute the success to his great fondness in helping others learn.

As the eldest of the three Dawson children, Paul often bored Len and his sister Carla to tears, trying to teach them from a play blackboard at home. Many times as a youngster he imagined himself at the blackboard before a classroom of eager minds - teaching clauses, prepositional phrases, and creative writing - his favorite subject. After college he anticipated with great eagerness his first teaching job. Little did he realize that teachers faced moments of crisis between jobs that paid little, along with remarks made by hardened educators intolerant of fresh ideas from a new teacher. After a time he eventually won the respect of many of his colleagues and especially his students. He only wished the paycheck was fatter.

Paul dragged a comb through his graying hair, thinking of Len and his successful career in the area of doctoring. Both parents had been impressed by Len's medical career over teaching, or so Paul thought. Twinges of jealousy nipped his heart, thinking of the money Len was bringing in as a practicing physician. Len's family occupied a large house in an affluent neighborhood while Paul must contend with the cramped conditions of a one-story ranch, overrun with everything that came with raising three kids. The boys shared a room while Karen had a room of her own. Both bedrooms overflowed with typical kid paraphernalia - sporting equipment, electronic toys, Barbie doll accessories, and an old computer system wired up in the boy's room. One day Paul hoped to afford a larger house if he ever became blessed with the finances.

He heard the voices of the kids calling for him and quickly strode down the hallway, depositing another kiss on his wife's cheek before heading out the door. "See you later, love of my life."

Katy laughed. "All right, have fun."

The kids were all over the van when Paul arrived and climbed into the front seat. A shouting match erupted as each one fought for the privilege of sitting in the prestigious co-pilot seat.

"Ladies first," Paul told the older brothers. Karen hopped into the revered seat, glancing with affection at him. In no time they were off, zooming around the stretches of highway. The boys chattered madly about a new television show. Karen peppered her father with questions about the game of football while they drove by houses scattered along the street.

Finally they pulled into the neighborhood Dairy Queen with the huge red logo sign. "Everybody out," Paul ordered.

The family trooped in and ventured directly to the counter where the kids ordered dipped cones and Paul a banana split. They had just settled themselves in a booth to enjoy the frozen treats when a young woman walked in, toting two little girls by the hand.

"Hey, there's Aunt Jan!" Dan shouted.

"Hi, Mary!" Karen waved to one of the little girls.

Janice came over and smiled at the family with ice cream dribbling down their chins. "This looks like a party. Where's Katy?"

Paul swallowed his portion before saying, "She's hard at work making the world's best spaghetti sauce."

"Her sauce is wonderful," Janice concurred. "One day she'll have to give me the recipe." Janice bent her head, appearing lost in thought before she remarked, "But I'm afraid Len won't be able to eat it right now."

At this, Paul peered up at her. "He's still having that pain? I remember you calling about it a few weeks back."

"Yes. He promised me he would go see a doctor, but...."

"C'mon, Mommy!" Mary and Lisa urged. "We want cones like Karen, Dan, and Pat!"

"Excuse me, I'll be right back."

Paul nodded, watching as she ventured forward to the counter to order the girls their ice cream. He could detect the worry outlining her actions and radiating in her voice. He remembered how Katy reacted when he needed his gallbladder removed. She accepted it like a trooper, despite the young children that needed her attention. Janice, however, was clearly concerned. Perhaps he could settle her fears by encouraging her to talk to Katy.

When they returned, Paul moved to another booth, allowing the cousins to share their ice cream together. Janice sat opposite him with a small dish of ice cream before her. She picked up the spoon and sunk it into the creamy mound, leaving the spoon embedded like a flag on the peak of a sandcastle.

"You do have a lot on your mind," Paul observed. "I don't know anyone who won't gobble down ice cream."

Janice shrugged. She stared at the ice cream tower for a moment before asking, "How did Katy take your gallbladder problem, Paul?"

"Like a pro," he admitted, spooning up the last chunk of banana, dripping with melted ice cream. "Katy doesn't worry about anything, to be honest. Nothing ruffles her feathers. She's like Mount Rushmore."

"Mount Rushmore?"

"You know - solid, dignified, never moving, the poise of a president even under intense pressure."

"Well, that's not me," Janice confessed.

Paul leaned back in the booth and folded his arms, observing her distress. "So you're really worried about this, aren't you?"

"I just can't get Len to go see the doctor. He promises to go, but he's too busy with the practice. His partner Mike had the flu, so Len's been covering all the patients. He drags himself home at night and just collapses into bed. He won't eat." Tears began to swim in her eyes. She took up a napkin with the Dairy Queen logo stamped on it to dab the tears away. "I don't know what to do."

"When the pain gets bad enough, he'll go."

Janice frowned. "That doesn't give me much reassurance, Paul. He's stubborn, you know. He tries not to let on when he has the pain. The attacks are becoming more frequent. He seems to be growing weaker."

Paul's eyes narrowed in concern. "Sounds bad. I wonder if I should give him a call?"

Her face brightened with his suggestion. "Oh, would you?"

"Sure. The problem is - Len and I don't communicate. It took you two women to knit our families together. If Len and I were single and on our own, I doubt we would even stay in contact."

"Why is that?"

Paul shrugged as he played with the plastic spoon inside his bowl. "We were never close growing up. We kind of tolerated each other, like we do now. We both took separate paths with our careers. We have totally different personalities. Instead of opposites attracting, we only clash."

"I don't see why that has to happen," Janice countered. "You both are successful men with wonderful families and the blessings of God. Why can't you heal this rift between yourselves?"

Paul shrugged. "Honestly, Jan, I'm not sure. Maybe it's because I just don't want to put the effort into it right now. If Len is open to the suggestion, then I might try my hand in it. There are unresolved differences that go way back. I mean we used to fight over who got the best pair of sneakers, which one of us the parents paid more attention to, who got money for college, who got the used car after Dad bought another, the list goes on."

Janice shook her head, finally sampling the ice cream that had now become the consistency of a milkshake. "I wish you could clear up this problem," she said softly. "I'm so tired of worrying about his health and everything in-between." She rested the spoon once more inside the dish and bent her head. "I pray daily for God to heal Len. I need to keep my faith strong in all of this, not only for Len's sake, but for the girls as well."

"Jan, I wouldn't worry about it."

She snickered. "That's what Len says all the time. 'Don't worry about it, Jan.' It must be the famous Dawson line."

"Look, I'll give him a call and encourage him to seek professional help. That's all I can do."

"I appreciate it, Paul," she said softly before rising from the booth and gathering her girls close to her. Paul watched her exit the ice cream shop, then turned to his own kids who were busy pitching paper napkin balls at each other. "Hey, enough of that! Clean up that mess before we leave here."

The kids obliged and followed him out to the awaiting minivan. As he settled into the driver's seat and fastened his seat belt, he could not help but ponder the conversation that dredged up the difficulties between Len and himself. He knew Len despised him as the older brother. They both nursed personal grudges in one form or another. Paul resented the family's wholehearted support for Len's career in medicine, and the way they funneled money to medical school rather than a teacher's college. Yet Len always felt he needed to compete with Paul. If Paul received a B in math, Len strived to attain the A when he reached that grade level. If Paul became a standout in track in the long distance races, Len pushed himself in the sprints. Despite the differences in both their ages and characteristics, life itself had become a fierce competition between the two.

After dinner that evening, Paul stole away to the bedroom, informing Katy of an important phone call he needed to make. She did not question him, but only raised an eyebrow in curiosity. He went inside, closed the door behind him, and sat for a lengthy time on the bed, staring at the screen on the phone. He thought about just texting Len but realized that would not do. This needed to be personal. He prayed for wisdom in the conversation to come.

When Len's voice came over the phone, Paul felt a pang of apprehension jab him in the stomach.

"Hey there, I wanted to know how you're doing?" he asked cheerfully.

"Fine," came the short, stiff reply.

"Well, uh...," Paul began, hunting for the right words. "Look Len, I just wanted to tell you that we're kind of concerned about this pain you've been having."

"What's this 'we' bit? Did Jan tell you to call me?"

"No. This was my suggestion."

"And when did you both talk?"

"We ran into each other at the Dairy Queen earlier today. She's really concerned about you, Len. She wants you to go see a doctor."

"Well I certainly don't need big brother telling me what to do," came the sharp reply. "I'm a grown man now, Paul, in case you've forgotten. I can make my own decisions."

"Len, I'm not trying to make a decision for you. I'm concerned about the effect this is having on your family. Jan's trying to keep a stiff upper lip, but I can tell you, she's really worried."

"Thanks for telling me how Jan is feeling," he retorted. "I don't care to hear from another man about my own wife."

Paul sensed Len on the verge of terminating the conversation. "Len, wait a minute. We're family, you know. Katy and Jan are both part of our family. We're all supposed to look out for each other. Can't we just talk about this like rational human beings?"

"Look, I appreciate your concern, but I will handle my health and my family."

Paul felt his patience wane under his brother's caustic tone. "Len, I just don't get it. What's with you? Here I'm only trying to help and you're shoving me away."

"You're trying to control the situation as usual. You think you can tell me when to see the doctor and how to take care of the family since you're stamped with the label of an older brother."

"That's not true and you know it."

"It most certainly is. I won't forget how you tried to control me...why you even wanted to control the few friends I had. You ridiculed me in front of Chris, Nick, and all the rest, calling me diaper pants Len. I had no friends after you got done shooting off your big mouth."

Paul slapped his hand against his forehead in frustration. "Len, c'mon, that was twenty years ago! We were obnoxious kids back then...especially me!"

"I had a health problem that required a urologist to perform a...."

"I know you did," Paul interrupted. "It was a dumb thing for me to say. I didn't know any better, but now I do. Why rehash something this old? What does it prove?"

The silence on the other end was deafening. Finally Paul heard a noisy exhale, followed by the words, "Look, I need to get back to my family."

Paul's fingers tightened around the cell phone. "You know Len, instead of harping on the sins of the past, you ought to be thankful for what you've got. You got the degree Mom and Dad loved, you've got that great house with plenty of room and a great family. Why can't you be thankful for things?" Silence met his question. He checked the screen to see the call had ended. Paul tossed the phone on the bed and gritted his teeth. He could not comprehend why Len did not see his good fortune in life. Paul shook his head. "I just don't get it. He should be as happy as a lark, yet he's miserable. Why? What can be done to heal this?" He then recalled his own jealousy of Len. *And how can I get rid of the same bug crawling around inside of me?*

Chapter 4

Janice tried to stay focused on an article in a newsmagazine while sitting inside the doctor's office, but found it impossible. She set the magazine down and stared at the print on the wall opposite her that displayed soothing, earthy tones of blues and browns. The classical music playing in the background did little to settle her fears. After much urging, Len finally relented in his stubbornness and went in to have the pain in his abdomen evaluated. The doctor sent him over to the University Hospital for a battery of tests including CAT scan, a bone scan, blood work, x-rays and the like. All the diagnostic testing made Janice nervous, but she knew the practitioner was being thorough. She only hoped that once they discovered the problem with his gallbladder, Len would elect to have it taken care of immediately. Their marriage had suffered tremendously since the malady first inflicted him. Many nights she found him in the bathroom, hunched over the sink. When Janice tried to comfort him, he shooed her away. The rejection pricked her like the thorns on a rose.

To ease her depression, Janice poured herself into her girls and the cake decorating business, which had picked up with the approach of the Thanksgiving and Christmas holidays. It seemed everyone wanted a decorated cake for celebrations at home or in the office. After the interview with the journalist who printed a story about Janice's cake decorating in the local paper, Janice found business had doubled. Twice she invited Katy over to help her bake up the cakes while she decorated them. Katy's little girl Karen played with the other two girls while the women busied themselves preparing the cakes for eager customers. Janice enjoyed the time with Len's sister-in-law very much. She confided in her of the burdens concerning Len's illness, and found Katy to be understanding but resolute. "You've got to get him to the doctor, Jan," Katy would say as yellow batter dripped into the twin cake pans dusted with flour. "Don't let him do this to you. When Paul started having his symptoms, I made him go. I think I even had to threaten him."

"I may be at that point," Janice admitted, taking up the wooden spoon to lick off the sweet batter. She shook her head, waving the spoon in the air. "Normally I never taste the batter. I've made it a rule to leave the batter and the frosting implements alone or else I'll be looking for clothes in the plus department."

"It's okay to treat yourself to something that tastes good now and then," Katy told her, adding a smile that warmed Janice's troubled heart. "There's something about sweets that boosts your energy level."

"It's the sugar, of course," Janice told her with a laugh.

"You're right, but I think it makes us feel young again, like when we were kids, licking Mom's mixer beaters or the big wooden spoon."

"My mother didn't bake. She wouldn't cook either. In fact, I can't believe I didn't starve as a kid."

"Well there, at least you can enjoy a taste of childhood."

Janice looked up from her reminiscing to see Len emerge through the white door leading out of the examination rooms. His face was expressionless as he went over to the window to arrange for the billing. Janice wished she had gone in with him to hear the doctor's report on the tests, but Len insisted that she stay in the comfort of the waiting room. The independence enshrouding Len's actions unnerved Janice. She wished at times he needed her assistance instead of maintaining this air of bravery like a general in the midst of a fierce battle.

"So how did it go?" Janice asked as they walked out the door toward the car.

"I have to go for more tests."

"More tests? Like what?"

"Well, this test is more invasive. I'll need to spend the day at the hospital."

Janice's eyes widened when Len settled inside the driver's seat. "That sounds serious!"

"It's nothing, Jan. The doctor wants me to have a liver biopsy, just to check everything out, you see."

"A liver biopsy?" she repeated, watching the car pull into the city street and head for the bypass. "But isn't it your gallbladder?"

"He wants to rule out any other possibility." He went on to explain that the surgery would take place near Thanksgiving.

"Not Thanksgiving!" Janice groaned. "You know how we get together with my mother and...."

"I know, I know," he said impatiently, "but I thought it would be better to schedule it around the holidays when things at the office aren't so hectic. I only have one delivery that may go during that time, and Mike can handle any of my other patients if the need should arise."

"So what do they do during this biopsy?"

"They use a needle to aspirate some tissue for a more in-depth analysis." He staring out the windshield, oblivious to Janice's mounting anxiety. She wanted to shake him and tell him how he was scaring her.

"This sounds really serious."

"It isn't. It's nothing. It's really just to rule out..." He paused and shook his head, burying the thought deep within himself.

Janice often wondered about those silent words during the few weeks leading up to the biopsy. The girls were sad to hear that their father would be in the hospital. Both of them drew him get well cards and kissed him farewell before Janice dropped them off at Katy's. She then drove Len to the hospital for his admission work-up. On the way to the hospital they met Paul, sitting at an intersection in the minivan, sipping hot coffee out of a plastic travel mug. He rolled down his window and greeted them.

Janice said hello but Len kept his face averted with his eyes staring straight ahead. She explained that they were on the way to the hospital for Len's biopsy.

"I heard about it from Katy. Hope everything goes well, Len. We'll keep you in our prayers."

"Thanks," he muttered, focusing his attention on the scenery outside the car window. For the rest of the trip and even inside the hospital, Len remained mute. The hard lines running across his jaw, coupled with his lips turned downward into a frown, told Janice of his own struggles over the situation. Even when Janice kissed him farewell before he was prepped for surgery, the return kiss was dry, without emotion. Janice bit back the tears, watching an attendant roll Len away in a wheelchair, clad in a hospital gown. She prayed to God that the doctors would find out what was wrong so they could lead the normal life of a happy family once again.

After the surgery, Janice was allowed a quick visit with a groggy Len before they began monitoring him in the recovery room. Outside in the hall,

Janice met up with the doctor who said they would know the results of the biopsy within the week.

"Len wouldn't tell me why this whole thing was really necessary," Janice told the surgeon. "Perhaps you can tell me."

The doctor only joked, saying that physicians liked to think the best concerning their condition and refused to jump the gun. "We do the testing to make sure nothing is out of the ordinary. There's not much else to offer until the biopsy report comes back, Mrs. Dawson. I won't speculate on the findings at this point in time. You will find out everything you need to know during your husband's regular office visit with his physician." He went on with a list of discharge instructions for Len, including bedrest for twenty-four hours, checking the bandage at the biopsy site for any foul drainage or excess bleeding, and reporting elevated temperatures immediately. Janice nodded but could not settle the mounting confusion within her. No one seemed willing to come forth and tell her the truth. *Perhaps there really is nothing to this,* she reasoned. *Len's been saying it all along. They only want to rule out any other possibilities.* She paused. *But what other possibilities could there be?*

Len recovered quickly from the biopsy to Janice's relief, but remained thin, listless, and without any appetite. He kept a positive attitude as he spent more time around the house during the week leading up to the doctor's appointment. Mary and Lisa enjoyed the added attention he supplied. He even assisted in their schooling while Janice decorated a cake in the shape of a Thanksgiving turkey for an office party. When she set to work forming the turkey's feathery wings with brown frosting squirted from a pastry tube, the family circled the table to watch her work. They giggled at the whimsical face she had created with curious black eyes and sharp smile. On top of the turkey's head she fashioned a hat similar to ones worn by the Pilgrims. A crisp, white collar made of cardboard surrounded his neck.

"You do wonderful work, sweetheart," Len remarked, accompanied by lips that nibbled her cheek and eventually found their way to her own lips.

For Janice, the contact felt like a dip in mountain spring waters. It had been so long since she and Len had made love. Often when he returned from the office, exhausted by the day's events, he immediately climbed into bed without sharing a word. After the girls were tucked in for the night, Janice spent many long evenings on the couch trying to read her Bible or engage her interest in a Christian novel. Without Len to keep her company, the nights were lonely. Sometimes she would slip into the master bedroom and watch the rise and fall of his chest as he slumbered away, thinking of the many wonderful encounters they had shared during their marriage.

Now the attention she received stirred up a hope within her that everything would soon be back to normal. The next morning he would find out the results of the biopsy. When she mentioned it that night, Len shook his head.

"I' rather you not go with me to the doctor's office."

Janice's eyes widened. "But why? I'm your wife, for heaven's sake."

"I know that, Jan, but I want to go alone and speak to the doctor. It's better this way. Two professionals jabbering away, using medical lingo, would bore you. And you won't have to keep bothering someone about taking care of the girls. The appointment's in the morning anyway, so Katy can't watch them."

"Maybe my neighbor will be able to...."

"Jan, please?"

Finally she relented, trying not to let her disappointment show as they readied for bed. To her surprise, Len was energetic and they enjoyed a time as husband and wife with a love that Janice soaked into every part of her being. In the morning, she did not seem so bothered when Len took off for the doctor's appointment without her. Instead she set to work planning a nice intimate dinner for the two of them. Janice contacted Katy at work and found her willing to pick up the girls after her job and take them home with her while she and Len spent an evening alone. Janice took her girls to the grocery store around noon and bought the fixings for a special dinner. She decided on a main dish of stuffed chicken breasts, thinking that it would be mild enough on Len's stomach. Rice pilaf and glazed carrots in a special brown sugar sauce would make nice side dishes. She stopped by the bakery and picked up his favorite dessert - a cheesecake smothered in strawberries. Her heart thumped with excitement when she arrived home and began preparations. She knew Len would not be home for several more hours. He wanted to do the afternoon's schedule of appointments at the office after his trip to the doctor.

At four o'clock, Katy came by as promised to pick up the two girls. "Mommy's making Daddy dinner," Mary announced, "with candles and flowers and everything."

Katy beamed her approval in Janice's direction. "That sounds lovely. I think your daddy is one lucky man to have such a nice wife." Katy waved her hand. "Just give me a call when you want me to bring them back."

"Thanks so much, Katy. You're a blessing."

"What are families for? Bye."

Janice heaved a sigh, then returned to the kitchen to inspect the chicken breasts. Everything would be ready at five-thirty when Len was expected home. She set the table neatly with their wedding china, and found two crystal goblets. The flowers, arranged in her best crystal cut vase, brightened the room. When she was satisfied with everything, Janice walked into the living room and glanced out the window, anticipating Len's arrival. She made several trips back and forth to the kitchen to check on dinner.

Finally at five-fifteen she heard the car pull up. Her heart began to flutter like a schoolgirl on her first date. She checked her appearance in the mirror hanging in the hallway, and removed a thread from the dress she had chosen for the occasion. When Len came through the door, she ran into his arms and gave him a kiss. "Have I got a surprise for you!"

He brushed by her and headed for the bedroom.

"Len?" Janice followed him into the room. "What's the matter?"

"I'm tired, Jan," he said in a monotone voice, slowly unbuttoning his shirt with jerky motions.

"Here let me help you."

He turned away. "I just need to rest, okay? It's been a long day."

She blinked. "All right, but I made us a special dinner. Katy has the girls so I thought we could..." She paused when Len collapsed onto the bed, inhaling sharp sighs before rolling over on his side away from her.

Janice bit her lip, trying to stifle the cry creeping into her throat. When she retreated to the formal dining room to see the beautiful table set for an intimate dinner for two, she cried for a brief moment. *Oh, don't get so worked up, Jan,* she scolded herself, blowing out the candles. *Len will be fine after a little cat nap. You should have anticipated this instead of planning a meal right when he walks through the door.*

After an hour, Janice turned off the stove. The rice pilaf had formed an unrecognizable lump inside the pan. The chicken breasts had dried out, despite the foil she wrapped over the pan. At least the cheesecake from the bakery still looked scrumptious, hidden inside the plastic container within the refrigerator. Perhaps she could coax him into eating a little dessert.

Janice went to check on him. She opened the door and peeked in to find him sitting on the side of the bed, staring out the window. "Len?" she asked softly.

He turned and cracked a small smile.

"Are you feeling better?"

He shrugged. "I suppose. Sorry about what happened. The dinner smelled pretty good, but...well, I just don't feel like eating."

Janice came and sat beside him. Despite his age he appeared old to her, like a plant withering away in the hot sunshine. When she picked up his hand, it felt bony and cold as though it was not alive. "What did the doctor say?" she asked softly.

"Nothing. The usual."

"The usual? So is it your gallbladder?"

Len stared off into space, still and silent. Suddenly his voice sliced through the air. "No, it's not my gallbladder."

A spasm went through Janice. She inhaled a quick breath to steady herself. "What is it? Does he know what's causing your pain?"

There was silence for a moment before Len said in a forced whisper, "Jan, it's cancer."

Janice sat up. Had she heard right? Her voice cracked when she asked, "Len, did you say what I think you said?"

"Yes, you did. He...he wants to start me on chemotherapy tomorrow. He's sending me to the best oncologist in town. But Jan...I...."

"Oh honey," she cried leaning her head into his shoulder, allowing her tears to fall.

"Jan...he says it's terminal. He says I may have six months at the most."

Her head popped up. Her lips trembled uncontrollably. Nervous chills gripped her body. "N-No!"

The rims of his eyes grew red from tears. "I waited too long to get it diagnosed. It was my fault. I was so stubborn about it. Maybe there might have been a chance if I had gone earlier but...."

"No, there's always a chance," Janice interrupted, despite the tears cascading down her face. "I believe in a God who can make you better, Leonard. I know He can. It's not too late for God."

Len shook his head, despite the faith that sparked within her. "Jan, it's bad. The tumor's massive. Because of its size and the involvement within the liver, it's inoperable. The chemotherapy will only slow it and maybe give me more time, but that's it."

Janice continued to shake her head, even as the neck of her dress now became quite damp with her tears. "No. We're gonna beat this thing, Len. We have to beat it! We...we must beat it!" She then began to cry openly, tugging on his shirt, before holding him tightly in her arms. *God, please don't take my husband away!*

Chapter 5

"Mother, I'm fine, really I am." Janice glanced out the window to see the silvery flakes of snow falling from the sky, covering the ground in a delicate pattern not unlike the lace adorning her coffee table. She smiled at the pretty scene until her mother's stern voice brought her back into the conversation. "Yes, what were you saying, Mother? Len's tired these days, but he's still caring for his patients. Mother, you know I can't make Len quit. He loves his work." She paused, thinking of the cake she needed to get into the oven for a new customer.

"I know and he does take care of himself. He's a doctor after all. Uh huh." She paused, shifting the phone to the other ear. "Look, I really need to go. Uh, huh. Yes." She sighed in exasperation, looking at the batter in the bowl. "Mother, anything you pick out for the girls will be fine. I suppose Barbie dolls would make nice Christmas gifts. Yes, and dresses for Sunday. They grow so quickly." She tapped her foot, trying to figure out some way to hang up without insulting her mother when she heard the girls arguing the other room. "Oh Mother, I have to go. There's something up with the girls. Yes, I love you, too. Bye." She quickly returned to the baking, pouring chocolate batter into a prepared jellyroll pan and slid it into the oven, just as Lisa came running into the kitchen bawling.

"Mommy, Mary threw her doll at me! Ow, it hurt!"

Janice sighed in exasperation when Mary came hurrying in to offer her side of the story.

"I didn't throw the doll. I just kind of tossed it at her and she couldn't catch it."

Janice bent down and gathered them both into her arms. "Now girls, you have to stop this fighting. There's so much going on right now with Daddy sick and Mommy trying to keep the cake business going. Can't you just play nicely?"

Mary wiggled her way out of Janice's arms and raced to the window, jumping onto the couch in glee. "Look, it's snowing! I want to go outside and build a snowman."

"Mary, stop jumping on the couch." Janice sighed, tucking a strand of her brown hair behind an ear. During these times that tested her patience, she wanted so much to break down and give up. Instead she tried to keep herself strong for the sake of her family. She refused to let them see the fear that gnawed at her daily at the thought of losing Len. How would she live? What would she do? What about her girls and the house? When these anxieties surfaced, she would bring out her Bible and read about God's promises. She felt confident that it was God's will for her husband to recover. She spent time daily on her knees in prayer, claiming the promise of healing in the Scripture. *By His stripes, we are healed.*

As the days passed, Len continued to weaken. The cancer ravaged his body, leaving him but mere skin and bones. They ventured to the mall on a shopping trip a week ago to buy him new clothes after his pants and shirts sagged to the point that he looked lost in them. Janice was alarmed to discover that he had dropped two sizes from when they were first married. When she placed her arms around his waist, she felt the ribs pressing against her. His thick, black hair had succumbed to the effects of the aggressive chemotherapy. The girls would rub their hands across his shiny bald head, exclaiming how nice and smooth it was. Janice tried to maintain a positive outlook, but found herself bothered by his changing appearance. All of this weighed heavily on her, like a burden of bricks resting on her shoulders. Despite the Scripture, the numerous telephone calls from people at the church, and the love displayed by both Katy and Paul, she felt her soul flagging in despair under the weight of everything.

The door burst open and a weary Len dragged himself in, tracking snow into the hallway. Since his illness, Len had hired on another physician, easing his caseload to allow him a lighter schedule. Everyday Len went faithfully to the office despite the doctor's suggestion that he quit working to conserve his strength to fight the disease. Janice watched Len give the girls their customary hugs, then remove his overcoat to display arms as thin as toothpicks and billowing pants that hid his scrawny legs.

"Can I get you something to eat, Len?" Janice offered, knowing what his answer would be.

He shook his head, flopped into an easy chair, and propped his feet up on a stool. "I can't eat, Jan."

She sat beside him and lifted his bony hand in hers, kissing it gently. "Not even a bowl of soup? I heated up a can of alphabet soup for the girls' lunch."

He winced. A hand went to his stomach. "Just the thought of food makes me nauseated. You go ahead and eat. I'm just going to relax and take a snooze."

Janice sighed and rose to her feet, calling for the girls to come have their alphabet soup and grilled cheese sandwiches. The snow began falling with a greater intensity, frosting the bushes and trees in pure white. She stood watching the flakes spiraling downward from the cloudy skies, washing away her anxieties for a brief moment. In the corner of the family room, Len slumbered away in the easy chair. She was thankful he found a bit of solitude from his struggle with the disease. Many times he was up at night, pacing about the room, clutching his abdomen. He refused the narcotics prescribed for him, but lived on Tylenol to control the pain.

The oven timer rang, disturbing her thoughts. Janice hurried into the kitchen to withdraw the jellyroll pan and test the cake. The fragrant scent of chocolate filled her nostrils.

"What's that gonna be, Mommy?" Mary asked from her place at the kitchen table as Janice slipped the pan onto an awaiting coaster.

"A Yule log."

Lisa slurped down the soup from her spoon before inquiring, "What's a Yule log?"

"Well, it's many different things. This will be a replica of a log that people put in their fireplaces on Christmas Eve as part of a huge fire to warm up the holidays. The word Yule is also associated with the birth of Jesus. Jesus is the Person we rest in, and from there, grow in our walk with Him." Janice thumped her foot on the floor. "This house here rests on what's called a foundation. The men who built the house poured the cement first, then added cement blocks. The rest of the house is then built on top of the foundation. Without a sturdy foundation made out of cement, the house would sink into the mud. Jesus is like that. He is the foundation for our lives. If we don't have Jesus in our hearts, then the lives we try to build for ourselves will only make us fall in the mud."

Lisa giggled at the notion while Mary held her sandwich in two hands, listening to the description in interest.

"So the Yule log is like the foundation for a toasty Christmas fire. Without it, there would not be a fire, just as we would have no meaning in our lives without the birth of Jesus in the manger."

"Are we gonna have a Yule log?" Mary wondered.

"I think that would be nice," Janice remarked, lifting the delicate cake onto a towel sprinkled with confectioner's sugar. "We don't have too many fires. I think we should have a Christmas Eve fire with a Yule log and invite your aunt, uncle, and cousins to come over and share in it. Maybe we could make popcorn."

"Oh, goodie!" the girls exclaimed, clapping their hands.

Janice nodded to herself as she prepared the cream filling to spread on the tender cake before rolling it into the shape of a log. "Yes, that's just what we'll do. I know I need to make Christmas special for Daddy. I want it to be a time he'll never forget." She considered for a moment that it might well be Len's last Christmas before brushing the thought aside to concentrate on her work.

With the last squirt of the pastry tube, Janice stepped back to admire the completed Yule log while the girls licked the inside of the bowl covered in chocolate icing. For the finishing touch she added two tiny red berries to the holly spray on top of a woody knot formed by a swirl of icing. She then covered the creation with a plastic hood and entered the living room to find Len with one eye open, peering in her direction.

"Len, I have to drop off this cake at a customer's house. Would you mind watching the girls while I'm gone?"

"Do you think you should be driving in this snow, Jan?"

"I'll be all right. I must deliver the cake today. It's just over in Brighton, a few miles down the road. I'll be careful." She went and kissed his dry lips before striding over to the closet to shrug on her coat.

"Take it easy," he murmured before closing his eyes once more.

Janice stepped outside the house into a winter wonderland. She plodded through thick, glimmering snow to the car and thought about her childhood days with the snowmen she made from the sugary snow, complete with rocks for eyes and a long carrot for the nose. Normally she feared driving in such wintry weather, but she had little choice. Her customers could not be expected to wait. They needed the cakes at the special parties and dinners arranged during this festive time of year. A missed cake would spoil not only the party, but also the reputation Janice had built up in her business.

Forcing back her apprehension, Janice opened the back door and set the cake on the passenger seat. Her breath formed puffy clouds in the cold air while she swept off the snow from the windshield. Snowflakes covered her coat in a blanket of silvery white. *Lord, help me,* she prayed, entering the driver's seat. Slowly she negotiated the car along the snowy drive through the neighborhood. Children played in their front lawns, throwing snowballs at each other or racing down the driveways on their plastic sleds. Janice drove onto the main highway and flicked on the windshield wipers to help clear away the accumulation of snow and ice. After a few blocks she passed the neighborhood where Katy and Paul lived. She thought of stopping in to say hello, but not knowing how quickly the roads might deteriorate, she pressed onward until she arrived at the address in Brighton.

A woman stood in the doorway, sweeping snow off the front porch when Janice pulled into the snow-covered driveway. "Mrs. Dawson, I wasn't expecting you to deliver that cake in this kind of weather!"

"I knew you needed it," Janice said, retrieving the cake from the car.

"Come on in and warm yourself."

Janice entered the small house to smell the faint odor of smoke from a wood burning stove sitting on a brick hearth in the living room. Several children played a game together on the carpet. Janice followed the woman into the kitchen where she lifted the cover to reveal the cake.

"Why, it's beautiful!" she exclaimed. "You do have a talent!" She went over to her purse and withdrew her checkbook. "How much do I owe you?"

"Thirty-two," Janice said, shivering a bit from the melted snow on her hair that sent trickles of water cascading down the back of her neck.

The woman wrote out a check for forty and handed it to Janice. "Now you must stay for a cup of coffee. You look absolutely frozen."

"I really need to get back," Janice began, but changed her mind when she saw the pot of brewed coffee and sniffed the pleasing aroma. She sat down in the corner of the kitchen nook while the customer poured out two cups of coffee.

"So how did you ever get into the cake decorating business?"

Janice allowed the steam to warm her face before sipping the beverage. "I took a few classes when they offered cake decorating at the rec center. I spent time learning the skill, then began making cakes for a few friends. One thing led to another and the business took off on its own."

"I can see why," she observed, glancing at the Yule log. "Do you make cakes full-time?"

"I teach my girls at home and alternate cake decorating with their schooling."

"You home-school then? So do I!"

Janice smiled at the thought of sharing some time with a Christian woman. She relaxed and began conversing with her over many topics until the discussion veered to Len's illness.

"I'm so sorry to hear about your husband," the woman said, patting Janice's hand. "It's hard to trust God when things like this happen. But there is a reason for it. Although you might not see it right now, there is a reason He brings us through these painful times as a way of preparing us for the future."

"That makes sense," Janice agreed, thankful for her insight that strengthened her during this time. "But it's hard, watching him waste away to nothing. I've tried explaining these things to the girls, but of course they don't understand what's happening to their daddy." She sighed and added, "Sometimes I don't understand myself."

"Do you mind if I ask you his prognosis?"

Janice blinked. "The doctors aren't too hopeful," she admitted, trying her best to keep from crying. These days, her tear glands worked overtime in response to all the painful emotions swirling around within. "Len waited too long to see the doctor and that worked against him. They give him six months at the most." She added quickly, "But I believe God will heal him. The Bible says He will."

Janice felt the customer's hand grip hers in a warm hold. "I hope so too. But sometimes there are other ways that God heals. Sometimes He allows our loved ones to go home to Him as a way of healing their pain-filled days."

Janice withdrew her hand. "I don't believe that. God wouldn't call Len away when we need him so much. I can't raise two little girls by myself."

"I didn't mean to make you lose hope, Mrs. Dawson."

"Call me Jan."

"Jan. And you can call me Cindy. But I can tell you once that I was in a similar situation, only it was my favorite brother. He had a brain tumor, you see. I was convinced God would heal him. I took him to all the healing seminars, we laid hands on him for healing in our church services, I confessed Scripture every day as I prayed by my bedside." She inhaled a deep breath. "But he died. Yes, Spencer died anyway. After that, I turned away from God. I lost faith. I believed God was unloving and unmerciful. It took many people praying for me to convince me that God was merciful to Spencer by taking him home to be with Him for all eternity. Sometimes when we look at our own situation, we don't see God's big picture. But He knows the big picture. He sees beyond our frail, simple-minded understanding. I guess that's why God also put in the Scripture - 'Precious in the sight of God is the death of His godly ones.' If death is somehow precious to Him, then it must be all right for His children to die, even if it seems to hurt those of us who are left behind."

Janice listened to this as a pain-filled lump formed in her throat. She refused to believe that God's perfect plan for her family would be Len's death. She gulped down the sensation before stealing a glance at the clock. "I'd better get going. Thanks for the coffee."

"Thanks for the cake." Cindy retrieved Janice's coat from the closet and held it out to her.

"And thanks for the listening ear," Janice managed to say with a shaky smile, despite the doubts plaguing her. She felt her knees tremble as she made her way to the car, using her gloved hand to wipe away the snow that had accumulated since her arrival. "I've got to believe that Len will be healed," she told herself, slipping behind the wheel. "I'm not giving up, no matter what she says. God wouldn't leave me alone like this. He can't."

With her thoughts consumed by the conversation, Janice found it difficult to concentrate on the slick roads. The snow appeared to have collected in drifts on the roadways since the short time she spent at Cindy's house in Brighton. The wind howled, blowing the flakes across her windshield in a whirl of white. Panic seized her as she tried to see through it all. "God, help me," she prayed.

Suddenly Janice saw a red object dart out in front of her car. Her foot slammed on the brake, sending the car into a skid until it collided with a tree. Everything seemed to happen in slow motion despite the few seconds it took for the car to come to rest against the stout trunk. Janice felt herself scream during the impact, then her extremities shake violently as everything became deathly quiet around her. "Oh God!" she cried, glancing around. "What am I going to do?"

Voices soon called to her from outside the vehicle. "Are you all right?"

Janice rolled down the window to see an elderly man and women peering at her. "I...I think so."

"Oh dear, Sam, look!" the woman pointed. "She has blood on her face! Maybe we should call 911."

Janice felt her forehead, then withdrew her gloved fingers to see the telltale smears of red from the lacerations where her head slammed against the side window.

"You just stay right here," Sam instructed her. "I'm going to call 911."

"N-No," Janice called after him. "I'm all right. Please, don't call."

"You sure?"

"Yes, yes. Just help me try to get the door open."

He did so, tugging firmly on the handle until the door popped open. He offered her a gentle hand and helped her out of the vehicle. Once outside, Janice saw the extensive damage done where the car hit the tree broadside. "Oh God, why did this have to happen? Len will be so angry. We only bought the car a year ago."

A police cruiser came to a screaming halt and a gruff officer ventured over to inspect the accident scene. He fired off a series of questions to a dazed Janice who tried to recount everything that happened.

"We saw it all, officer," the woman and her husband interjected. "This lady braked to avoid hitting one of those kids who was sledding right in the middle of the road."

Janice turned to stare at the woman. "I did? I remember seeing something red, but...."

"Yes, that was our next door neighbor's son, Larry. He'd been sledding down his driveway most of the afternoon and going right out into the middle of the street. We thought it was too dangerous, and now look what's happened."

Janice glanced up the road to see the tire tracks in the snow where she braked to avoid hitting whatever she saw in the roadway. The mere thought that she had missed striking a child sent her into another wave of weeping, until the stern voice of the officer interrupted with more questions.

Janice supplied the answers as best she could, hiccuping in the midst of the explanations. When the police officer asked if there was someone who could pick her up, she glanced at her surroundings. "Where am I?"

"Oak Avenue."

"Oak Avenue. Oh, I'm right near Katy and Paul. Please, can you take me to 305 Hickory Street? It's only about two blocks from here. I have family there."

The policeman obliged, escorting Janice to the cruiser after she retrieved her handbag from the car. *Don't I have enough heartache to deal with already, God?* Janice thought, watching the falling snow bury the crippled car.

"Mom! Dad!" Dan cried as he ran into the foyer of the house, covered in snow from sledding down the front lawn. "There's a police car coming up the driveway!"

Katy and Paul stared at each other in bewilderment before dashing to the front porch to see the cruiser crawling through the mound of snow. The bedraggled form of Janice emerged from the back seat.

"Jan!" Katy cried, ignoring the snow falling on her hair and clothing as she raced out to meet her. "What happened?"

"I-I had an accident," she sniffed.

"Oh, you poor thing," Katy crooned, wrapping an arm around the shaky form. She assisted Janice to the house where Paul waited with the door open. They gestured her to the living room sofa. Karen came out of her room to investigate the commotion and stared wide-eyed at the sight of her aunt's face bloodied by lacerations.

"Karen, run and get the first aid kit, will you?" Katy instructed. "And Paul, go make up some hot tea."

"I-I shouldn't have gone out," Janice mumbled, shaking her head. Pink tears fell, staining the front of her sweater. "I was delivering a cake. I knew the family needed the cake."

Katy smiled her thanks to Karen who presented her with the small plastic case, then stepped back to watch while Katy opened the box containing the bandages and antiseptic.

"It's terrible out from what we've been hearing on the news," Katy observed. "I've seen the plow come by only once today. They're calling this thing a genuine blizzard."

Paul returned with a cup of steaming tea. "You take sugar or milk?" he asked.

Jan shook her head as she sipped the warm beverage. "That tastes good. Oh, I can't believe this happened. Len will be so upset. I think I totaled the car. I won't know until a garage inspects the damage."

"The most important thing is that you're safe," Katy told her. "You can always replace a car.

Janice winced when Katy gently swabbed the wounds on her face with a cotton ball dipped in antiseptic. "The witnesses...the neighbors, they said I missed hitting some child on a sled." She set the cup on the table and burst into tears. "Oh Katy, what if I had hit someone else's child? I would never be able to live with myself!"

"Jan, you didn't hit the child. Don't think about what might have happened. Be thankful that you are all right and so is the child."

"I guess."

"Do you want me to call Len and tell him you're here?" Paul offered.

Janice's eyes widened. "No! No, don't tell him about the car. I'd better go on home now. He's probably wondering what's happened to me. Can you take me, Paul?"

"Jan, you just got here," Katy began, "and I think you need time to recover first before...."

"No, I've got to get home," she interrupted, bolting to her feet and looking around for her coat. "Len isn't well. I left him home with the girls so I could make this delivery. I was only supposed to be gone an hour at the most. Now it's been over two."

"It's no problem, I'll take you," Paul offered. "C'mon."

"Be careful," Katy said softly to Paul as he pulled out his parka from the hall closet.

"You know I will." Paul gave her a kiss before following Janice into the storm.

The drive was cloaked in silence for most of the trip. Janice stared out the window of the minivan, watching treetops covered in snow sag in remorse. Paul tried to think up some witty comment to lighten the moment, but decided against it. Instead he chose to tell her how much his family was looking forward to spending Christmas Eve at her place. Janice mumbled something to the effect that she was looking forward to it as well.

"You don't sound like it," he commented. "I mean, well, I guess I shouldn't be surprised. You've been through quite an ordeal today."

"Every day is an ordeal."

He cast her a glance, noting the look of depression that overshadowed her. "How's Len doing with the chemotherapy?"

"He's lost his hair and he won't eat a thing."

"That's hard to believe," Paul remarked. "Len loves food, or used to anyway. He was always the first one to the table whenever Mom had dinner ready. He wouldn't even stop for the prayer, but used to dish up half the potatoes and meat on his plate. Sometimes Carla and I would have to tell him to save a little for us starving kids."

Janice said nothing, leaving Paul angry with himself for not coming up with something better than painful reminders of the way Len used to be. He chewed on his bottom lip before deciding to chat about the Christmas holidays, which he knew Janice loved. He talked about the gifts the kids were hoping to receive under the Christmas tree, and how he wanted Janice's opinion on a sweater he had picked out for Katy. In no time they had arrived at the house to find Len standing in his bathrobe in the doorway, flanked by the girls. Their faces displayed anxious looks.

"Jan, what happened? I was worried sick."

"She had a run-in with a tree," Paul intervened, helping Janice out of the van into the snowy drifts bordering the driveway.

"A tree? Oh no! I don't believe it. You see, I told you not to go out in this kind of weather. What were you thinking anyway? And what about the car? Don't tell me the car's totaled. There goes my insurance rate right through the roof and right when we have all these other bills to pay."

Paul cast his brother a withering look. "C'mon Len, lay off. Jan's just been in an accident. Aren't you the least bit thankful she's okay?"

Len glared at Paul with a look that could have melted the snow. "There you go again, acting like the big brother know-it-all, trying to tell me what I can say to my own wife!"

"And there you go, caring more about your own personal problems without showing the least bit concern for someone else."

"Get off my property!" Len shouted, grabbing Janice by the arm and propelling her into the house. "As far as I'm concerned, I don't care if you ever show your face around here again! And that includes Christmas Eve."

Chapter 6

Janice felt miserable in the week following the accident. While the effects of the cancer raging through Len had taken its toll physically, the car accident seemed to have driven him into a pit of bitterness where no one could reach him. With Christmas Eve approaching, Janice pleaded with him to make up with Paul so they could have a nice family gathering as planned. Len refused. Instead he threw out outlandish comments toward Janice about the day of the accident, including raw accusations about her and Paul. Janice sat on the couch late one night, unable to sleep as her mind reverberated with his comments.

"Yeah, ol' brother Paul seems to be sticking up for you a lot lately, hasn't he?" Len snapped. "Why is that, Jan? Is there something going on between you two that you're not telling me?"

Janice cringed when she recalled the stinging accusation that lanced her heart. "How can you even say such a thing!" she cried back. "Katy and Paul have both given their hearts away to us during this time."

"Yeah, Paul sure is giving his heart away, isn't he? It doesn't surprise me. I know you don't consider me a man anymore now that I'm bald, emaciated, and can't support you in my profession. I guess anyone, even a married man, would be better than me."

Janice blinked her eyes as the familiar flow of tears once more came calling. Reaching for a tissue to blow her nose, she thought of the many boxes of tissue she had gone through over the course of the last few months - mourning Len's condition and now the tongue lashing that hurt worse than anything she had ever known. She realized she could no longer speak to Katy and Paul again without making Len suspicious. She leaned her head against the back of the couch, trying to draw strength from God during this time. Right now He seemed so far away. Alone with her thoughts, Janice tried desperately to understand Len's behavior. She knew the cancer must be devastating to him, not only physically but emotionally as well. She encouraged him to go to church, but he refused, claiming he would not be made a spectacle by his appearance. Janice suggested a toupee or even wearing a hat, but he only scoffed at the idea.

"I'm better off here," he only told her, burying his face in his tablet.

Besides Len's temperament, Janice also noticed a change in their two daughters. Both Mary and Lisa had become quiet, keeping to their rooms whenever Len was in one of his bad moods. When Janice tried to talk to them about their father, the girls only stared at her in confusion and bewilderment, looking forever like two lost lambs searching for stability in their home.

All these things weighed heavily on Janice. She glanced over at the phone, wishing there was someone to confide in. The only person that came to mind was Cindy whom she had given the frosted Yule log during that snowy winter day. Despite the late hour, Janice picked up her cell phone and scanned the contact list until she found Cindy's contact number.

A sleepy voice greeted her. Janice almost hung up until she felt the gentle nudging in her heart.

"I'm so sorry to bother you at this time of night," Janice began. "I'm Janice Dawson, the lady who made the Yule log cake."

"Oh yes, I remember. The cake was delicious. We got rave revues during our Christmas party."

Janice managed a small smile before launching into her difficulties concerning Len.

"It doesn't surprise me at all."

Janice arched her eyebrows. "It doesn't?"

"No. You see, when a person is dying, they go through certain stages. I'm not much into psychological mumbo jumbo, but I do know in the Bible, especially if you read Job, there are stages one goes through in accepting tragedy in their life. Your husband is going through a particular stage. First there's denial. Then questioning. Now it seems he's going through anger."

"So this is normal?"

"It's normal," Cindy assured her. "My brother went through the same stages. You won't believe the huge lies he concocted about my family."

"Oh, I do know!" Janice was quick to say, sitting up straighter in her seat. "Len has even gone so far as to think I'm having some kind of affair with his brother! Paul and Katy have tried to be so supportive of the family and me. But Len doesn't see it that way. He dislikes Paul so much, and now he thinks...oh, I can't even say it again. If I do I'll just start crying again, and I've already gone through two boxes of tissues this week alone."

Janice could sense Cindy nodding her head up and down in comprehension. "It's all right to cry, Janice. Crying is an outlet God has given us. You don't need to be ashamed of it. Even Jesus cried after his friend died. It's the shortest verse in the Bible, but probably the most meaningful. God certainly understands the need to mourn."

Janice sensed a soothing balm pour over her wounded soul at these words.

"But on the other hand, you must not give in to your husband's anger either. This may sound like I'm being mean and insensitive, but you're going to have to lay down the line with him. You can't just go off by yourself and get miserable whenever he does this to you. Firmly deny his accusations and try to keep your determination. If he thinks he's getting your goat, it will only feed his anger. You must stay supportive, but you do not need to support his anger just because he has cancer."

"In other words, don't let my sympathy fall over into his anger."

"He doesn't need sympathy, either. He needs support, but most of all, he needs the strength of God."

Janice sighed. "That's another problem. He refuses to go to church."

"Maybe you could have the pastor come talk to him at the house."

"That's a good idea. I can invite the pastor over for lunch, then slip away with the girls somewhere. Now that most of the snow's melted, I think I can get out. I really do need to finish up my Christmas shopping."

"I think the effort will be worth it. I know this is a difficult time, and I really do understand. I'll keep you both in prayer, okay?"

"Thanks." A small smile of peace creased her lips.

"And Janice?"

"Yes?"

"Call me anytime, day or night. The moment you sat down at the table with me and started pouring out your heart, I felt that somehow God had knitted us together. I want you to know that I'll be there for you, okay?"

"Th-thanks, Cindy. That means so much, just to hear those words. I've kind of clung to Len's sister-in-law, but now with these accusations flying, I don't dare talk to her."

Cindy sighed. "Remember what I said, Janice. You have to go on with your life. If you feel the need to talk to her, then talk to her. Don't let your husband's anger rob you of that time. If you want to get together, then do it."

"I want to have their family over for Christmas Eve."

"Then have them over. It might prove to your husband that there is nothing going on between you and his brother. Plan on it and let me know what happens."

"Okay, and thanks Cindy." When Janice hung up, she felt as if a hundred-pound weight had been lifted from her shoulders. Despite what was happening in her life, she knew that God cared about her circumstances. He sent her the right person who could help in her time of need. Sensing a renewed confidence, Janice strode off to bed, her mind already planning the Christmas Eve party with Paul, Katy, and their children.

Janice had just finished arranging the Christmas cookies in an attractive pattern on one of her best silver trays when the doorbell rang. Mary and Lisa ran to answer it and laughed in glee when Paul and Katy entered, their arms laden with presents. Pat, Dan, and Karen followed. They all exchanged hugs and joyful exclamations of Merry Christmas when Janice came out, wiping her hands on a tea towel decorated with holly and berries.

"Merry Christmas," she said to Katy, giving her a hug. When Paul opened his arms to embrace her, Janice only smiled meekly and offered her hand. He glanced at her with raised eyebrows, then shrugged and shook her hand.

"Merry Christmas," he said. "Where's Len?"

"He wanted to rest before everyone got here."

"Let me tell him we're here," Paul decided before Janice stopped him.

"I...well, I'll go get him when it's time," Janice whispered, supplemented by a weak smile. "He's been kind of edgy these last few weeks. He really wasn't up to the whole party thing, but I thought it would be good to have the family here celebrating."

"I think it's a great idea," Katy assured her. "Oh Paul, go bring in the goodies. I made up a few finger foods."

"I got to help Mommy spray the cheddar cheese into the slices of salami," Karen told her cousins in glee.

"They're hors-d'oeuvres," Katy explained. "We also have crackers and a cheese ball."

"Sounds delicious." Janice glanced over at the boys who were roaming around the living room, checking out her decorations. They included several antique nutcrackers, a nativity scene decorated with sprays of fresh pine that gave off a sweet scent, little angels perched on their pedestals, and finally an old mechanical Santa Claus in a worn red flannel suit, clasping a brass bell in one hand.

"This looks like it runs on batteries," Dan commented, lifting up the ancient Santa to see the battery compartment underneath.

Jan smiled. "Here, let me show you." She hurried to retrieve some D cell batteries out of a drawer and insert them into the feet of the Santa Claus. "Now Karen, push the little black button there."

Karen did so. Immediately the Santa's eyes glowed red. His arm moved up and down, ringing the bell while his head turned. A scratchy voice cried out cheerily, "Ho, ho, ho, Merry Christmas!"

All the children laughed.

"Where did you get that?" Paul wondered, his eyes lighting up in amusement like the Santa Claus who continued to ring his bell while staring at the onlookers through beady red eyes.

"It belonged to my family. It must be at least thirty years old."

"Hold on to it, Jan," Katy said. "I'm sure it will be an expensive antique someday, especially since it still works."

"The girls always like to see it every Christmas, don't you Mary and Lisa?"

The two girls nodded while sharing laughter with their cousins over the Santa's antics.

After a bit, Paul asked if everyone would enjoy playing the game, Win, Lose, or Draw. "It's similar to the game of Pictionary," he explained, "but for this, we can use the blackboard in your classroom. We'll draw pictures on it and the team has to guess the picture in the shortest time possible. You have a blackboard I presume, right Jan?"

"Oh yes," she said, walking back into the room. Paul followed her. "You see it's just fastened into the wall with screws. You can take them out easily enough and then screw the board back in."

"You don't mind?" he asked.

For some reason Janice felt tense standing there with Paul observing her. Memories of Len's accusations filtered through her mind. She glanced away, keeping her eyes trained on the blackboard. "I think it will be fun."

"Okay, I'll go ask Len where he keeps his tools." He walked off whistling as Jan went over to the mirror to acknowledge her flush cheeks.

"God, please help me," she prayed, staring at her reflection. "I feel so uncomfortable around the family and Paul, especially after the lies Len had concocted. I don't know how I can get through this evening without Your help. Please, somehow, help our two families, and please, help Len and Paul reconcile this night of all nights when you brought your only Son to live here among men. Amen."

Paul walked upstairs with a steady foot, his hand brushing the side rail. He squinted in the dimness of a hall bulb that had gone out. Cautiously he approached the door, opened it, and stared at the figure lying on the bed, reading on an IPad. Inhaling a deep breath, Paul watched the figure, wondering how this man could be his brother. The bald scalp shone in the light generated by the swaying bulb. Even from this vantage point, he could see how the disease had eaten Len away. He winced, recalling their past conflicts, wondering if there was some way to put aside their differences before it was too late.

Paul thrust his hands into the pockets of his corduroys. "Hey, Len," he called out.

Len looked up over the tablet. "Oh, I didn't know you all were here." He returned his attention to whatever he was looking at.

Paul cleared his throat. "Hey Len, I uh...I thought you'd like to know we're getting ready to play the game, Win, Lose, or Draw."

"So what," Len muttered.

"Remember we used to play it all the time when we were kids?"

Len shrugged.

Paul paused, wondering how to proceed. Finally he asked Len where he kept his tools.

"Down in the basement, at the work bench," Len told him.

"Look, we really want you to come join us."

"I don't think I'd be much fun."

"Well you're sure not helping yourself by acting like a hermit. Why don't you come and be part of the family? It will make you feel better, guaranteed."

Len again stared above his tablet, his eyes glaring. "Look, I didn't invite you here. My wife did. It's her party. Have fun, but I'm warning you to stay away from her."

Paul stepped back, startled by the comment. "What do you mean - stay away from Jan?"

"You know what I mean."

Paul marched up and stood before Len. "No, I don't know what you mean. Just what are you trying to say?"

"I'm saying I know what's been going on. Don't think you can hide things."

"Hide what? What are you talking about, Len? If you don't shoot straight with me right now I'll...."

Again the glaring eyes of Len met his. "I mean you've been chasing after my wife, that's what I mean! All these innocent little meetings - driving her around, calling her on her cell phone for secret little chats."

Paul staggered under the weight of the accusation. He felt the heat enter his face. "Are you out of your mind? There are reasons behind every one of these so-called meetings. The call was to set up the time for the party and..."

"Sure, there's excuses for everything."

"...most of which," Paul continued in a steady voice, despite the shaking of his limbs, "centered on you! Look, whether you like it or not, you're not the only one suffering from this illness. Everyone else is suffering too. I know you got a bad break in life, Len, but what's the sense in making everyone else just as miserable as you?"

Len's fingers gripped the sides of the tablet until his knuckles showed pure white through the tight skin. "You have no idea what I'm feeling."

"You're right, I don't. I've never had cancer. But I can see how it's ripping everyone apart, including Jan. I know you don't deserve the cancer, but she doesn't deserve your attitude. All Katy and I have tried to do is be supportive in this, which also includes supporting your wife. In case you didn't realize it, I happen to be a happily married man. I have no designs on your wife, nor will I ever. All I've tried to do is help." He whirled and headed for the basement stairs. "But I can see that our help has only been a bother. I'm taking my family and leaving right now. Merry Christmas, Len."

His feet pounded the stairs as he ran up and burst into the living room. Everyone stopped and stared at his abrupt entrance. "C'mon, we're leaving," he said roughly, grabbing the coats off the steel hangars hanging in the closet.

"What?" Katy cried, casting a glance at Janice.

"Get the kids, we're leaving," Paul snapped. Then to Janice, he said, "I'm sorry things turned out this way, Jan, but you won't be seeing us again."

Janice stood in the hallway, gaping in shock. Her hand pressed against her chest to calm the streaks of pain coursing through her heart. Katy threw her one pitiful look before following her husband and children out into the cold, blustery night. Mary and Lisa both tugged on Janice's arms with tears rolling down their cheeks, asking why their uncle, aunt, and cousins had to leave so soon. Janice could only comfort them with a hug of reassurance. "Tell you what," she told the two girls. "Let's have Christmas a little early and open the gifts your aunt and uncle brought over. Would you like that?" The flow of tears subsided, replaced by cheerful expressions and eyes bright with anticipation.

Colorful wrapping paper depicting Santa in his sleigh gave way to twin baby dolls that could be fed and changed. Janice looked over the dolls with her girls and tried to smile, but sensed a disturbing ire rise up within her. She knew something terrible had unfolded between Len and Paul in the basement. It seemed Len had again succeeded in controlling the situation, even when Janice had tried to pursue her Christmas Eve plans.

In determination, Janice asked the girls to dress in their nightgowns for bed. After she had tucked them in and whispered prayers with each girl, Janice inhaled a breath and entered their bedroom. She stared at his bald head, wondering what thoughts raced through his mind. Did he indeed battle anger and helplessness as Cindy had suggested? If so, how could she deal with it? She knew she could not handle these burdens alone. Her attempts at having the pastor come over from the church to speak with him failed when

Len refused to meet with him. Without the comfort of God during this time, she knew Len struggled alone with the disease. In his weakness, he chose to fight with whatever strength he possessed, rather than with the strength of Christ.

In her distress she whispered a prayer to God for wisdom. Her extremities relaxed and her heart slowed from its rapid beat. With soft steps, she approached her husband.

"Go ahead and bawl me out if you want," his voice snapped, "but I didn't tell Paul to leave. It was his decision."

"I'm not going to bawl you out, Len," she said, nestling in a chair next to him. "What are you looking at?"

Her question sent him looking at her in puzzlement. The tense wrinkles of hostility creasing his face slowly relaxed. "Well...I...I'm looking at pediatric diabetes," he said, showing her the tablet screen. "There's been some new discoveries."

Jan began reading the medical jargon concerning the illness before asking him if the journal was helpful.

"Yes, there are some diagnostic techniques in here that I would like to pass on to Mike." His voice softened. "Thanks for asking."

She rose to her feet and extended her hands. He sat up then and she kneaded away the tension in his neck. She felt him stiffen under the touch at first until the rhythmic massage began to work their magic, loosening the muscles of his neck and shoulders.

"That feels good," he murmured, slowly relaxing under her touch. After a moment, he asked, "Jan, do you still love me?"

She bent and placed a loving kiss on the side of his face. "I love you with all my heart."

"Even with all this?"

"Len, I love you with everything in me. But I know that God loves you more."

Len rested quietly, thinking on those words. "If that's true, then why am I going through this?"

"So He can show His love for us. How can we really see God's love and care if everything was hunky dory? We wouldn't. We would be praising ourselves for our fine lives, our good jobs, our secure homes." She came and knelt down next to him, leaning her head against his shoulder. "But it's during these times, these hard times, that He's strong. When we are weak, He is strong." Janice clasped Len's frail hand in hers. "I think God wants to show us how strong He can be in all of this, Len. We've been trying to do it in our own strength. You've been trying to cope with your illness in your strength, and I've been trying to do everything that needs to be done, including feeding the emotional hunger in both you and the girls. But I found out tonight that I can't do it alone. I've got to have God help me."

Len stared off into space for a few moments. "I suppose as a physician I've tried to handle this myself. I mean, I'm supposed to cure people. Why can't I cure myself? I feel frustrated over the inability to get rid of this thing inside me, invading my tissues like an army, taking away everything on the inside and on the outside. I've thought many times that only God can really heal me, but I figured there was something left that I still needed to do." His hand reached out to tousle her brown hair. "But more than just losing my profession or even my life, I-I don't want to lose you or the girls." Tears pressed out of his eyes and drifted down his cheeks. "You mean everything to me. I know I haven't shown it these last few weeks, but it's true. I can't lose you."

"We're right here, Len," Janice told him before gently placing a kiss on his lips. "We're always here for you." He returned the kiss with eagerness, his arms enfolding her in an embrace as they whispered to each other, "Merry Christmas, my love."

Chapter 7

Winter seemed like it would never end. The snow continued to fall, piling up around the house like an entrenchment of pure white until the family could barely see out the front windows. A solid lump of white sat in the driveway where the last of their vehicles now stood. Janice was thankful for her store of canned foods in the pantry. Her heart raced at the thought of attempting to drive in this kind of weather. Occasionally she had Paul go for a few items, which he left on the porch without saying a word. When Janice tried to get Paul to reconcile with Len after the confrontation in the basement on Christmas Eve, he shook his head and folded his arms in defiance.

"I have nothing to say to him," he said stiffly.

Janice tried to enlighten him about the stages of acceptance in end stage cancer. "You must know he's afraid, Paul," she pleaded. "He's afraid of losing everything. He's already lost his job and his physical features. Now he's afraid of losing what's most precious to him, his family. Can't you see that this might be the reason behind his lies?"

Paul only brushed away the explanation. "I don't care what he's feeling. In my book, there's no excuse for him to accuse me like he did, no matter how sick he is."

Janice could see the wounds ran deep. She took the matter to prayer, but found no solution waiting in the wings. Len refused to call Paul to offer an apology and Paul would not speak to Len. The rift between the brothers seemed as irreparable as the cancer ravaging her husband's body.

During the long winter months, Janice turned the living room into a convalescent room as Len continued to weaken. A wheelchair occupied the foyer. Len took all his meals there when he was not in bed. Most of the day he simply slept, trying to conserve the energy remaining in him. Janice watched his color turn from the normal Dawson hue of healthy brown to a dingy yellow, signifying the effects of the cancer on his liver. His legs began to swell from fluid buildup. Janice had to wrestle his legs into tight stockings each day to help assist with his circulation. Some days she would have to feed him meals when his hands shook. The only thing she was thankful for during this stressful time was his sharp mind. Occasionally his colleague Mike Free would come visit and explain certain cases, asking for his opinion. Janice noticed that these times in particular seemed to impart vitality into his deteriorating condition.

With the snows of winter burying them in their little house, coupled with Len's frail condition, Janice found herself cooped up like a chicken in a hen house. There were days she merely stared out the window, wishing that she could fly away and escape. Sometimes she thought about a trip to sunny Florida, roaming the beaches and picking up seashells while the warm waters off the Gulf of Mexico caressed her toes. Other days she imagined herself shopping in the mall for a new outfit or trying on the newest scent of perfume out on the market, anything that might rid her mind of the hardship of this life. Likewise the girls grew fretful, whining constantly and clinging to her like frightened mice. They soon tired of their Christmas toys and winter itself. They walked around the house in circles with their fingers tracing along the walls, asking Janice what they could do. Janice tried to make their classes interesting, but she noticed they were falling quickly behind in their lessons. Many days the girls would not do their work at all, but simply stared out the window, watching the snowflakes float down from the skies, adding to the millions of flakes making up the pile of snow that covered the ground.

Finally when Janice thought she couldn't take it anymore, the phone rang. It was Katy, telling her that Paul had decided to take the kids ice-skating at the new skating rink downtown. "And he wants to take you all."

"You know that Len can't...."

"I know, but I don't skate. I had a bad fall when I was a teenager and haven't been interested since. I was thinking that I could watch Len and you can go along with Paul and the kids."

Janice clutched the phone. Instantly she felt her heart pound inside her chest. "I-I can't do that, Katy."

"Why not?"

"Well, I uh...well...oh, I don't know how to say this, Katy, but...."

"Look Jan, I know what Len told Paul on Christmas Eve. You and I both know it's only the illness talking. You shouldn't be afraid to have a good time with your nephews and niece. I mean, we're family."

Janice exhaled a sigh of relief when Katy said these words. In eagerness she agreed to the plan.

"Wonderful!" Katy said happily. "On Sunday the pastor shared with us about Jesus washing His disciples' feet. I know we haven't done too much for you all in the last six weeks, especially after the whole Christmas episode. This is just a small way to let you know that we care about you."

Janice burst into tears when she heard this. "Thanks, Katy. I was really starting to lose it here. The girls haven't been right at all. I don't dare go out of the house with all this snow, especially after that accident."

"It's no problem," her soothing voice responded. "What are families for but to take care of each other? That's the lesson I learned from this Sunday's message. My kids want to do something, too, and Paul was getting pretty itchy with school being cancelled all the time. So this gives everyone something else to do besides moping."

"But are you sure you want to take care of Len?"

"Yes, I'm sure, so long as it's not heavy duty."

"No, not really. He sleeps most of the time anyway. He also enjoys fiddling with his IPad."

"Then it sounds like I shouldn't have any trouble. We'll be by in about an hour. Oh, and be sure you and the girls dress warmly."

When Janice ended the call on the cell phone, she felt her spirits soar into the clouds, far above the troubles of this world. She now scurried around the house, assembling warm clothing for her girls who broke into rounds of smiles when she told them the news.

"But I don't know how to skate," Lisa complained.

"None of us do," Janice said, helping them into their pink long johns. "But this is the fun of it. We get to learn something new."

"And who's going to take care of Daddy?" Mary asked.

"Aunt Katy will," she said as her hope increased. *Perhaps this whole idea might be an answer to my prayer. Maybe Katy can smooth things over with Len while I enjoy some time away. Oh thank you, God.*

Janice was grateful that Len remained asleep when the relatives arrived. She explained to Katy all that might be required in her absence, supplemented by a list of medications Len was to take in the middle of the afternoon, and the doctor's phone number in case of an emergency. Janice wiped a hand across her forehead as she glanced around. "I hope I didn't forget anything."

Katy patted her arm. "Don't you worry about a thing," she said. "Paul has his cell phone if something comes up. You just relax and have a good time. You deserve it."

Jan inhaled a breath and thanked her profusely for arranging all of this.

Katy winked. "It's our pleasure, isn't it Paul?"

"Sure thing," he said easily.

The skating rink downtown was crowded with youngsters and adults alike who took the opportunity of time off from work or school to enjoy a day of skating. Cheerful laughter filled the air when Paul pulled the minivan into a parking space. "Okay, everyone out!" he said in a jolly voice as he stood below the sliding door to offer a hand to the little girls. Dan and Pat were already racing over to the booth to try on skates.

Janice peered out the door of the minivan to see the ice glistening in the sunlight, and patrons whirling away on steel blades to a classical tune filtering through the speakers. "This looks wonderful!"

Paul held out his hand and helped her down. "We usually go a couple of times during the season," he explained as they walked over to the booth. "The rink just opened last year."

Janice opened a coat pocket to fish out the money she had tucked inside, but Paul firmly placed her hand back into the pocket and shook his head. His dark eyes twinkled. "My treat."

"Thanks. C'mon Mary and Lisa, let's find some skates for ourselves. You come too, Karen." Karen tagged along as they walked into a huge shed where skates were stacked along the shelves in various sizes, with white for the ladies and black for the men.

"Can I help you with sizes?" a woman asked.

Janice fingered her chin. "I take an adult eight. Lisa is a thirteen and Mary takes almost a two. What size shoe do you take, Karen?'

Karen shrugged.

"You're probably the same size as Mary. If it's wrong, we'll try the next size."

The woman promptly retrieved the four pairs of skates and returned with them. "Just take these to the counter and show them your ticket. Check the skates back here when you are finished."

"Thanks." Janice smiled, feeling like a schoolgirl again as she flung the skates over one shoulder and approached the large bench bordering the rink where Paul and the boys were already lacing up their skates. She set to work placing her girls' feet into the tight fitting skates as the boys chattered about participating on an ice hockey team someday.

"Ice hockey!" Paul repeated. "I don't know about that."

"Why not, Dad?" Pat was saying. "When you get to be thirteen, they have this junior league. I'll be thirteen soon."

"Well," he huffed, tightening his skates, "we'll have to discuss this aspiration with your mother. Quite frankly, I don't imagine she'd be too keen on the idea." He glanced up, watching Janice struggle to lace Mary's skates. "Did Katy tell you what happened to her as a teenager?"

"She said," Janice paused, tugging on the laces before firmly tying them, "she said she fell or something."

"Not only that but she busted her leg."

Janice looked up. "She did?"

"Broke her leg right here," Paul pointed to the mid-section of the tibia. "Had to wear a cast for two months straight. Ever since that time, she won't skate or ski or do any of the winter sports. Now me," he paused, standing to his feet and extending his arms to steady his balance, "why I love sports. Take me down a fast mountain ski trail or on a skating oval - woo wee, I'm in all my glory!"

Janice could not help but giggle, watching Paul stumble his way out to the oval like a drunken sailor. With a firm stroke of his skate that sent ice splinters flying in the air, he glided across the sheen of ice that sparkled in the noonday sun. Soon his boys were chasing him around the oval, deep into their own game of tag. They laughed and yelled, all the while chasing each other, stumbling over their skates and sprawling stomach first onto the ice. Janice cringed as she watched them, then turned to the party of girls lined up behind her. "We'll just take this nice and slow," she assured the girls, helping them each onto the sparkling ice so they could get a feel for the strange terrain on their sleek skates. No sooner had Lisa stepped out onto the ice when she fell down on her backside with a terrific thump. Instead of crying, she stared up at Janice in surprise.

"Are you all right, honey?" Janice asked anxiously, helping the little girl to her feet.

Lisa nodded before placing a mittened hand in hers. With short glides of their skates, they skated around a small section of the oval while Karen and Mary were having fun growing accustomed to their skates. After a time, Paul skated by, grabbed up Lisa in his arms, and whisked her away.

"Uncle Paul!" she cried in glee, beating playfully on his chest with her tiny fists.

"Skating away!" he sang, twirling her around on the oval. She giggled and laughed before Paul deposited her safely beside her mother. "Who's next?" he asked breathlessly.

"Me! Me!" shouted Karen and Mary. Paul picked up Mary next and skated away with her before returning to gather up his own little girl in his arms.

"You're going to be exhausted after all this," Janice commented, watching him heave for oxygen as he took off.

"Yep, but there's no better exercise," he huffed.

Janice could only shake her head, trying to imagine Len whirling around with the girls in his arms. She recalled the one time they rented roller skates before they were married - an event that proved disastrous in the end. Len had skated in his past, but Janice never had, and ended up colliding with everyone on the rink. She left the rink embarrassed, along with bloodied knees to boot, and vowed never to put skates on again--roller skates, ice skates, or otherwise. Now she laughed at the white skates on her feet as she took small strides on the ice while keeping her arms extended for balance.

Suddenly she heard the whoosh of skates behind her and a firm hand pressing against her upper back, pushing her along the ice. "What! Who's there?" Then she heard a familiar masculine chuckle. "Paul, don't. I'm trying to get used to this."

"I'm just giving you a little speed. You're as slow as a tortoise."

"Well, pardon me!" Janice said with a small grin.

"I'll show you how to skate in pairs." He placed on hand behind the small of her back and took up her hand in his. "Now skate with me. Ta, ta, dee, dah," he sang.

She followed his lead and found herself easily gliding along the ice with his short firm strokes. All the cousins stopped to watch them move swiftly in and out of the crowd until they came to rest before the children.

"Hey, you looked pretty good out there," Dan said.

"Your aunt's a natural at skating," Paul winked before collapsing on a bench. "But now I'm bushed, so you all go and have fun."

The children obliged, each taking off at their own pace. Janice watched Paul as he bent over to tighten his skates, deciding this might be a perfect opportunity to speak with him. She cautiously took a seat at the end of the bench. "Thanks for the lesson."

He glanced up. "My pleasure. I had fun. You sure you haven't skated before?"

"I'm trying to remember. I think I did once or twice, but my memory's kind of fuzzy. I was thinking about the time when Len took me roller-skating. It was a disaster." She shook her head, then glanced out at the skating oval as the children whizzed by, laughing. "This is so much nicer. I think it's even easier."

"Some say that."

"Where did you learn to skate so well?"

Paul leaned back against the wire mesh fencing behind him and crossed his arms. "I skated quite a bit when I was younger. Len and I used to play ice hockey on the pond near where we lived."

"What fun!"

"I suppose. We played on opposite teams. We were always in competition, it seems." He grew quiet, suddenly lost in thought.

"Actually Paul, that's what I wanted to talk to you about," Janice began.

He cast her a raised eyebrow in curiosity.

"Look, I can see you and Len don't get along very well. I'm just wondering if it's possible, well, if you could somehow reconcile with one another."

Paul blew out a sharp sigh. "I've wanted to in the past, Jan, but Len doesn't. It takes two, you know. He has a lot of unforgiveness."

"What about you?"

Paul shuddered as though shocked by an electrical bolt. "I suppose I do," he said reluctantly. "I was mad that everyone loved Len for going to medical school and becoming a doctor. Dad and Mom gave him money and everything. I had to work to pay for my education. Everyone thought teaching was for sissies. They called it a woman's occupation."

"That's nonsense."

"I know it is, but as an impressionable young man, the comments cut deep. I guess I never got over them. So you could say we both have some unforgiveness and probably some jealously, too."

"I'm praying you both will be able to work this out," Janice said. She then offered in a cautious voice, "You see...I know, well, I know that recently Len has been making some outlandish accusations and...."

Paul shifted uncomfortably on the bench. "I'd rather not talk about that if you don't mind."

"I think it's good to talk about things. I know how terrible I felt before Christmas when everything in my life was falling apart before my very eyes. I found a nice woman to talk to. She was a customer of mine and she seemed to understand. I felt much better after I was able to open up about what's going on inside."

"Len had no business whatsoever coming out with what he did. I mean, we can't even be a family and do things...well, like this for instance," he paused and waved his hand across the ice rink, "without thinking it's improper."

"It's like what Katy said. It's just the disease talking."

"I know that's what she says but...."

"It is, Paul," Janice pressed. "Len is upset with his appearance and everything. He doesn't work anymore but lays around at home, trying to get through each day. Think what it would be like if you had no hair, no strength, and could no longer provide for your family."

"I'd be pretty bummed," Paul admitted, kicking his skate into a hunk of snow.

"That's what he's going through. Despite what he says, I'm trying to show him my love. The Bible says that love covers a multitude of sins. So if Len is telling these lies, I'm going to still love him and help him through this."

Paul looked over at her. "You're one tough cookie, Jan. You once told me you don't have the strength like Katy, but you do. You two might be different in some ways, but you both have spunk. And anyone who dares to skate with a lughead like me is brave to boot." He rose to his feet and extended his hand. "So how about one more glide around the oval before we get these hungry kids some pizza?"

"Sure!" she agreed enthusiastically, settling at once into a rhythm as they sped around in time with the music.

When Janice arrived home with the children, she was surprised to find Len in the kitchen, preparing dinner. Katy beamed in delight, giving Janice a wink of encouragement before hustling herself out to the awaiting minivan. Janice promptly told the girls to change out of their clothes and into something warm before going to see Len. She found him standing over the stove, stirring a kettle of stew.

"You haven't cooked in ages," she said, rubbing a hand across his bony shoulder as she sniffed the hearty aroma of the boiling stew.

"I have an appetite for once," he confessed, "and I had a hankering for stew. I thought it would taste good to you and the girls after being outside in the cold."

"You want me to finish it?"

"No, you go and relax. You've been acting like a slave around here as it is. I want to do this for you."

Janice planted a kiss on his cheek. As she did, she noticed his abdomen bulging beneath his sweater, which she had never seen before. "You look like you're putting on weight."

He shook his head. "It's not extra weight," he told her softly.

"What is it then?"

He added a cutting board filled with sliced carrots into the thick mixture of gravy bubbling in the pot. "It has to do with the cancer. The fluid starts building up in the abdomen."

Janice stepped backward and shook her head. "Isn't there anything that can be done?"

"I'm on the Lasix, you know, which helps with the water retention." He added, "No, not really. It's end stage liver cancer."

"Oh, Len."

He turned and gathered her into his arms. "Hey, it's going to be all right. I'm feeling okay at this moment, Jan. Let's just enjoy this evening and put the cancer out of our minds. Can you do that for me?"

She nodded her head and wiped the tears from her eyes.

"Did you have a good time skating?"

"Yes."

"I'm glad you went. After spending time with Katy, I can see that I've been really pigheaded these last few weeks. I don't know what got into me. I couldn't see that my brother and his family were only trying to help you and I. Can you ever forgive me?"

"Of course I can. I-I love you so much, Len."

"And I love you too, sweetheart."

Chapter 8

"But I want to go," Mary pleaded when Janice put on her sweater and checked her appearance once more in the mirror.

"Honey, I'm afraid you can't. Nana's going to stay here with you."

The little girl stared up into the hard eyes of her grandmother, Lucinda Harris, who towered over her. She shook her head and clawed at her mother's pants. "Please, Mommy, please let me see Daddy!"

Janice kissed her girl on the top of her head. "Now Mary, I let you see Daddy just the other day. He's still the same, but today the doctor put him in isolation. Only grown-ups can see him now."

"What's isolation?"

Janice drew in a breath. "It's a special room where you must wear protective gowns and gloves so Daddy won't get sick. You see, if he got sick right now, it could hurt him bad." She glanced up, hoping for some measure of warmth from her mother. Lucinda only shook her head with her arms folded before her.

"Do they really think that's going to keep out the germs?" Lucinda wondered. "I hear about hospitals, how they're full of germs and everything else. Some walk out sicker than when they entered."

"I don't know, Mother." Janice heard the toot of the car horn, signaling the arrival of Katy and Paul. "There they are, I have to go. Now you girls mind Nana, please. I won't be too late." Janice could see the look of sadness emanating in her daughter's eyes, but thrust it aside and hurried outdoors. The air was scented with the flowers of springtime. Tulips and daffodils put forth their showy display. When Janice found the flowers in bloom, the mere sight of them gave her hope that after the dreariness of the winter, God had brought forth a restoration of the earth. She prayed the same would happen with Len. Yet a few days after the plants blossomed, Len was sent to the hospital with pneumonia. In a week the doctors transferred him to the isolation ward until he regained his strength. Janice hoped he might recover enough to come home in time for Easter. She had circled the day in pen as a reminder of the miracle when Christ died and rose again, thinking how wonderful it would be to witness a similar resurrection of healing within Len's frail body.

Inside the van, Katy and Paul greeted her. Janice sat in the rear seat watching the couple. Since the ice skating adventure, the two families met on different occasions for a night of games or just to chat. Len would participate in the gatherings until his illness forced him to remain in bed, with only short periods out in the wheelchair to break up the monotony of the day. Janice was grateful to see Len and Paul on speaking terms again after the misunderstandings that clouded the winter months.

They arrived at the parking garage with the sunlight reflecting off the white siding of the massive hospital. Janice hopped out of the van and made her way through the visitor's link with Katy and Paul lagging behind, their hands clasped tightly together as if drawing strength from each other. When they arrived on the medical unit, a nurse showed them how to apply the gowns, masks, and gloves required of visitors to Len's hospital room.

"I never thought I'd see the day when I'd have to wear a dress," Paul joked in a strained voice while Katy assisted him with fastening the gown. "Look at this get-up." He performed an awkward curtsy before the two women.

Janice couldn't help but smile behind her mask.

"It's for Len's protection, you," Katy said, swatting him with a pair of gloves. "Now don't forget to put this mask on."

Paul placed the mask over his face, then raised his thumb and forefinger. "Ah ha, now I'm a bandit! Hand over your money, ladies. I wonder if criminals ever considered parading around like this." His laughter reached a loud crescendo that sent Janice glancing curiously at him, wondering what prompted his strange humor at a time like this.

She ventured into the hospital room and pulled back the curtain to find Len sitting up in a chair, his head resting back, his eyes shut. She tried desperately to force back the tears at seeing his frail condition. His sallow skin color reminded her of a ripened banana. His eyes appeared sunken into the bony sockets of his face. Beneath the gown and the lap robe he wore, she could see the bulge of his abdomen from the accumulation of fluid, and farther down, his legs swollen to three times their normal size. Shaking her head, Janice cleared her thoughts concerning Len's outward appearance to concentrate on the real man that she loved with all her heart.

A moan of despair suddenly pierced the air. She whirled to find Paul dashing from the room - the gown he wore fluttering behind him. She left the room to find Paul, still draped in his gown, standing at the far end of the corridor. He leaned heavily against a metal railing running along the wall.

"Oh God," he moaned, shaking his head.

"Honey, what's the matter?" Katy asked, rushing to his side.

"Katy...Len looks...he looks so..." He paused when he saw Janice. "I'm sorry, Jan. I shouldn't be doing this. It's hard enough without me acting like a...."

"You're only human, Paul," Janice said softly. "I guess I'm used to Len's appearance. But you haven't seen him since he's been here. I understand."

Paul wiped a gloved hand across his face as if to clear away the terrible sight he had just witnessed. "I had no idea how bad he is. This is awful. The cancer has...why...he's gonna die, isn't he? Oh God, my brother's going to die. I can't believe it."

"We don't know that," Katy answered, trying to calm his grief. "Please, Paul," she whispered, "not in front of Jan."

Janice slipped away after hearing these words. The finality of Paul's statement clouded her eyes with tears. "God can still heal him," she stated matter-of-factly, regaining the strength to return to Len's bedside after changing into another gown. She sat next to Len and took up his cold hand in hers. "God's going to heal you, Len. He must. He has to. I can't lose you. I need you."

Len's eyes flicked open at that moment. He struggled to raise his head as if the mere effort used what little strength remained within him. A small smile creased his lips. "Jan."

"Hi, honey."

"You...you look funny."

"It's the mask," she confessed.

"Please, can I see your face? I-I miss your face."

"But Len, I'm not supposed to...."

"I'll risk an infection just to see your lovely face," he whispered.

Janice glanced around for any nurses that might be hovering near the door. With no one in sight, she lifted the mask and watched the smile broaden across his sickly face.

"You're beautiful," he said, lifting a forefinger to caress one silken cheek. "You are so beautiful. How fortunate I am to be married to someone like you."

"And I'm so glad I married you, Len."

"I-I believe you. I really do."

Janice replaced the mask and reached forward to gather his frail form into her arms. "Oh, my poor darling," she murmured before praying over him for his healing.

Len released her and shook his head. "No, Jan."

"No, what?"

"No, there's no hope for me now...in this life anyway."

"Len, with God there's always...."

"I want you to know that I talked with the hospital chaplain today. He's a very godly man. H-He helped me to...to see things...things that I've been hiding in my heart for so many years. I wish...I wish I could say them."

"You can, honey."

"No...not to you. I-I have to say them to Paul. It's Paul who must hear them, but he's not here."

"Yes, he is," Janice corrected, generating a look of surprise on Len's face. "I'll get him for you if you want me to."

He straightened a bit in his chair and smoothed out the blanket covering him. "Yes...yes, do that."

Paul was still standing in the corridor, conversing with Katy, when Janice approached. "Paul, Len wants to see you."

"He's awake?" Katy asked.

"Yes, and he wants to talk to you Paul. Please?"

Paul hesitated, glancing from one woman to the other. "I don't know if I can."

"Please go," Katy told him, gently ushering him down the hallway. "Please, Paul."

Paul relented and made his way back to the room. He stood for several minutes beyond the closed curtain, wondering what words he could say to a man so close to his eternal rest. Finally he gathered up his courage and stepped forward. "Hey, Len," he greeted feebly.

Len waved him over. "Thanks for coming. Please, sit down right here."

Paul did so, keeping his eyes trained on the oxygen set up just beyond the bed. The very sight of Len in his debilitated state sent ripples of anxiety coursing through him.

"I-I had the chance to speak with the hospital chaplain today," Len said slowly. "I see now that I've been wrong in many areas, and a big area is you."

"Now Len...," Paul began.

"No, hear me out. I've always been jealous of you as the older brother. You set such a fine example for the family. I-I felt I had to make these huge strides just to keep up with you. I know I felt some sense of satisfaction when Mom and Dad favored my education over yours. But I was jealous at how you overcame obstacles on your own. You had a determination to make it in this world, no matter what."

"Len, I...."

"And yes, maybe I have been successful in my career and could afford a fine home. But you are richer than me in so many ways, Paul. You have a love for God that is your foundation. I-I have never been a strong Christian. I played the Christian game to placate Jan, but I never really believed it." He inhaled a sharp sigh. "But the chaplain helped me realize my error."

Paul felt tremors grip his limbs. His lower lip began to quiver. "Len...," he began.

"I want to ask for your forgiveness. You...you've tried to help me and care for me, as an older brother should. I was blinded by my own selfishness. I wanted to make it big in the world. I-I was jealous of your perseverance. You didn't depend on the praises of others."

Paul bent his head as watery tears filled his eyes. The feeble figure before him wavered like ripples on a lake "Len, I'm so sorry about all this. I'm sorry for the years I wasted not getting to know you better. I thought you had it all with the praises of the folks, the money, and a fine family. You have been blessed. I was the one who had a jealousy problem. I was shortsighted. I didn't see that God was choosing to bless each of us in His own way." He rose awkwardly to his feet. "I don't know if it's right, but could I...."

"Please," Len offered, extending his pencil-thin arms that wavered in the air.

Paul fell into the arms, hugging the fragile form. The mask he wore dampened with his tears and his hands began to sweat inside the rubber gloves. When they parted, he felt a renewal inside him as though a miracle had taken place within the room. "You will receive your reward, won't you?" Paul softly asked his brother.

Len nodded. "Yes. Even though I'm not worthy, Jesus made me worthy. I think I will see Him very soon."

Len went to be with the Lord not a week after the tender meeting between brothers. Janice received word late one night when the nurses called to tell her of his critical condition. She and Paul drove immediately to the hospital, but arrived too late. The nurse told them of Len's passing and inquired if they would like to see him. Janice nodded. Her tears overflowed onto Paul's shoulder as together they walked into the room. Len appeared peaceful in the bed against the pure white of the sheets, his face serene, his muscles relaxed. They stooped down beside him and kissed him good-bye, knowing he was enjoying the peaceful bliss of heaven with the Lord. Janice stumbled out of the hospital with tears gushing forth like geysers from her eyes. Paul's hugs of reassurance did little to ease the torment brewing inside her heart and a soul that cried, *Why did You let him die, God?*

The pain within her intensified as preparations began for the funeral. The house filled with mourners - those in the family practice where Len worked, along with family and friends from church. Len's parents arrived to help with the funeral arrangements. They appeared old and forlorn to Janice, with pure white hair and wrinkles etched into their dark faces. From their expressions and the tears they shed, the death of their son hurt them as much as it did her. Len's sister Carla arrived as well, dressed in the fancy suit of a city dweller used to living in the business world. Janice's mother proved cool and collected around the visiting in-laws who invaded her domain. She shed no tears at her son-in-law's passing, but only buried herself in work - cleaning the house, freezing the multitude of casseroles that came pouring in from sympathetic neighbors and friends, and handling the deluge of calls inquiring of the funeral arrangements.

Janice was thankful for the support of the church and the pastor who assisted in arranging the service that took place several days later. First came the visitation at the funeral home. The arrangements of flowers surrounding the walnut casket were from all walks of Len's life, from fellow students during his days in high school, to a college professor in medical school; from patients he had cared for and distant relatives. Roses decorated the top of the casket along with the gold cursive lettering that spelled out *Husband* and *Father.* The sweet scent of the flowers added to the sadness brewing within her. Janice felt as if she had been transported into an empty world without a future. She stood stiffly next to the casket of her husband, dressed in a drab black pantsuit that her mother disliked. She grabbed hold of the hands of the mourners, thanking them for coming. Once or twice she shed tears with those who offered her a hug of sympathy.

During the funeral service, she sat stiff like a marble statue with her girls by her side. She tried to listen to the pastor as he spoke of Len's devotion to the family and his practice, and his love for God that assured him of a final resting place in eternity. Yet she could only stare at the casket, thinking of Len resting inside the satin covered lining, dressed in his pinstriped suit. With her fingers knotted together on her lap, she wondered how this could be happening to her at such a young age. At the cemetery, the feeling was the same. She sat immobile in one of the folding chairs erected by the funeral director while Len's casket lay on metal rollers, ready for burial once the mourners left. Again the pastor read Scriptures that fell on deaf ears. All she could think about was Len's suffering and his final retreat into a place she knew so little about.

When all the formalities had concluded and the relatives departed, Janice collapsed wearily onto the couch. The house seemed still without Len there. The wheelchair sat in the foyer, Len's tablet on the table. With a stiff, mechanical jerk of her body, Janice came to her feet. She went over and turned on the tablet, looking at the last pages Len had scanned before going to the hospital. One of the open pages was the Bible and words about heaven. Instead of joy, mourning overwhelmed her, bringing with it a sickening a pain that melted her insides. Would her mourning one day turn to laugher as Scripture promised? When Lucinda returned from tucking the girls into bed, Janice was still there, weeping and wondering.

"Now Janice, you can't bring him back," her mother said. "It's over. You must go on."

"I know," she gasped, wiping away the tears.

"You must think about what you're going to do about the bills and living in this big house."

Janice turned off the tablet and resumed her place on the sofa. "Len's insurance will cover things for a while," she said, fumbling with a loose button on her blouse. In a sudden burst of frustration, she yanked it off.

Lucinda stared at her. "Why did you do that, for goodness sake? Let me sew that back on for you." She retrieved the sewing box, opening it to reveal assorted thread and needles. "Take the blouse off."

"I don't want the button sewn on, Mother," Janice informed her through gritted teeth. "I wanted to do it." She sprang to her feet and began pacing the carpeted floor like a lion caught in a cage. "I feel like I want to break something...a vase, a jar, anything to release what's inside me."

"You're acting foolish. You've got to get control of yourself."

"Me, a widow at age thirty-three. Who would've thought such a thing!" Janice whirled and pointed at the dark outfit clinging to her skinny form. "Me, a widow with two girls. What am I supposed to do with my life now, Mother?"

"You're going to have to learn to live again. I had to. You will learn."

"Learn to live again," she echoed, standing before the mirror in the hallway to peruse her blotchy skin and bloodshot eyes from a day of weeping that now continued within the confines of her heart. "How can I? How can I possibly live again?"

Chapter 9

Janice stirred in another packet of sugar while staring at the classified section on craigslist, having forgotten the two packets she'd already dumped into the lukewarm coffee her mother fixed a half-hour ago. When she sipped the sugary liquid, she winced. Empty packets lay strewn across the counter. "How many did I put in there?" she wondered to herself. Janice reached over and gathered up the packets, wadding them up into a ball and tossing it into the trash. Such things seemed to be happening at frequent intervals. Just the other day she noticed a strange odor in the car when she drove the girls to the playground. Upon opening the hatch, she found a bag of spoiled food she had forgotten to bring in after a trip to the grocery store. Another time she forgot about paying the monthly bills until late notices began arriving in the mail. When her mother turned on the faucet to do up the dishes one evening, a trickle of water greeted her.

"Janice, did you pay the water bill?" Lucinda asked, placing her hands on her hips.

Janice clattered down the stairs to Len's desk. Her fingers fumbled nervously through the plastic letter carrier where she kept the monthly bills. "Water bill, water bill," she mumbled to herself. Her shoulder muscles tensed with the stress, sending pain shooting into her skull. "Oh God, am I going insane?" Finally she discovered the bill tucked in with the rest of the late payments. When she returned upstairs to inform her mother, Lucinda huffed about in anger.

"Really Janice, you're going to have to get your mind down here where it belongs. Not only don't we have any water, but you'll have to pay the extra charges to have the meter turned back on."

"I'm doing the best I can!" Janice shouted in a tone that sent the older lady storming off into her room. Janice squeezed the bill between clenched fingers before falling onto the couch in the living room, holding her head in despair. How could she possibly cope with all the things that needed to be done, including the bills, the upkeep to the home, the expenses left over from Len's medical care, not to mention caring for the girls. Everything seemed to be tumbling down on her at once, like an avalanche of responsibilities that crushed her with its weight.

Now as she threw the coffee down the sink, Janice wondered if she really had lost her mind in the midst of these trials. Perhaps she should seek professional counseling. Her mother harped constantly on her moodiness since Len's passing. When Paul and Katy came for visits, they expressed the same concern over her change in personality. Six months passed before Paul finally coaxed her into taking back the wheelchair to the medical agency where Janice had rented it. When Katy suggested that she remove Len's personal belongings from the house and donate them to a local charity, Janice raced for the closet and threw herself in front of the door. "Don't you dare touch his things," she hissed, as though Katy had suggested the most hideous act imaginable.

Katy's tender eyes widened in response. "Honey, I just want to help you get your life back together."

"I want Len's things here."

When Katy walked into the bathroom and saw Len's shaving accessories out and his bathrobe hanging behind the door, she shook her head in confusion. "What's all this?"

"I-I like having them out."

"But Jan, Len's with the Lord now," Katy gently reminded her.

"I know that!" Janice spat back. "Can't I have reminders of him now and then? Or am I just supposed to just forget he ever existed now that he lies in some coffin, buried ten feet deep?"

Since the outburst, Katy and the family rarely came to visit. Janice mourned that day, thinking what a crazed woman she must have appeared to a family who was only trying to help. Now she sat at the kitchen nook and scanned the classified listing for a job that might offset the bills. Len's life insurance would help for several years, but Janice knew she must do something about their financial situation before the money ran out. Since Len's passing, Janice allowed the cake decorating business to collapse. She sold most of her bakeware to help buy needed items for the girls. When her mother agreed to take over the schooling of the girls and the regular household duties, Janice focused her sights on obtaining some type of job outside the home. Scanning down the list of positions available, her eyes landed on an opening in a bakery in town. Immediately she dialed the number.

That evening, Janice felt a resurgence of confidence after landing the job at the bakery. When the proprietor remembered hearing about her cakes from satisfied customers, a job was instantly offered. Janice bought presents for the girls and a bouquet of flowers to decorate the dining room table. Life was finally smiling on her for a brief moment.

"Entering the work force is not as easy as you think," Lucinda commented, placing food on the table that night.

Janice unfolded her napkin and plopped it on her lap. "Mother, even your comments are not going to affect me tonight. I'm glad about the job. It's the first decent thing that's happened in my life in almost a year."

Lucinda glared. "Since you have your life back together, maybe I should just move out. I can see that I'm no longer appreciated here."

Janice felt a slow anger rise up within her. "I just wish that for once you could say something nice. I know you've helped me here. I couldn't have done it without you."

"Maids are much more expensive."

Janice let the comment go and bowed her head to offer up a simple blessing for the food and her job. She did not notice the moodiness surrounding the girls during dinner. Both of them picked at their meatloaf and green beans, even after Lucinda shouted at them to start eating. Finally Lisa gave up and went to cuddle the doll Janice had given to her that night.

"Aren't you going to do something about this, Janice?" Lucinda asked, pointing her fork at the girl.

Janice sighed and went to sit beside her daughter on the couch in the family room. "What's the matter, honey?"

"I don't want you to go to work," she said, sniffing.

"Oh honey, I have to work. We need the money."

"I don't want you to work. Daddy went to work at the hospital and he didn't come back." She stared at Janice with eyes brimming in tears.

The remark stung like the prick of a thorn. Janice never considered what Len's death must have seemed like through the eyes of her two young daughters. "Sweetheart, I'm going to tell you the truth. Daddy's work in the hospital had nothing to do with his sickness. You know he was very sick with a mean bug that took over his whole body. I know it's hard to understand.

God decided Daddy should be with Him in heaven instead of here with us. I know we'd rather have him here, but God wanted him there."

Lisa threw herself into her mother's arms. "I miss Daddy," she sniffed.

Janice held her close, feeling the tears smart her eyes. "I miss him, too."

Every day Janice went off to work to the bakery and enjoyed the fulfillment of creating her own cake decorations where an employer praised her work. She looked forward to entering the establishment with the pleasing smell of sugar, allowing her mind to concentrate on decorating cakes rather than dwelling on her own private thoughts. Yet the tensions of life were always waiting for her when she walked in the door. One evening the children asked if they might attend public school come next fall. When Janice sat with her mother to discuss the girls' comment and what might have spawned it, Lucinda only shrugged her shoulders.

"They don't do their work, Janice," she said. "It's obvious you didn't teach them good learning habits at home. I think you should put them in the public school system, especially since you feel you can no longer stay here with them."

"But Mother, don't you see what I'm trying to do? I'm trying to keep this home going while providing for the family."

"A woman's role isn't to play the man of the house," Lucinda fired back, her eyes glazed with anger. "I had to play the man in the house when your father walked out on me. I know what it did to me." The angry fire in her features gave way to the emotion she had kept concealed for so many years. "I had to go off to work, leaving you all by yourself. It nearly tore my heart in two, watching how you changed. I knew you and I were drifting apart, and I couldn't stop it." The emotion turned into a flood of tears that cascaded down her wrinkled cheeks. "Now I see it happening all over again."

"Oh, Mom," Janice cried, leaning over to give her mother a hug, realizing she had not used the affectionate title of mom for her mother in years. "I had no idea how you felt."

"I kept it cooped up inside, just like you're doing. I found out over the years that it's left a big scar in me. I don't want the same thing happening to you. You're going to have to heal, Janice, and you're going to have to let some things go. If you don't, you'll end up old and bitter like me, and with girls who will resent you for the rest of their lives."

That evening, Janice took a walk by herself around the neighborhood to contemplate her mother's words. She recalled the painful times during her teenage years and how she wished her mother was at home instead of tackling two jobs to make ends meet. Yet she wondered how she would manage everything if she did not hold down some kind of job. "She's right, though. I do have to let things go. It just isn't the same anymore. Maybe I'll just forget about keeping the house, for one thing. It's too expensive to maintain anyway." Her boot kicked up a chunk of snow leftover from a snowstorm several weeks ago. A cold wind nipped he cheeks. It was a winter like all winters, drenched with pain and a multitude of questions. When would she ever enjoy a winter of blessing and healing?

She paused to view a neighbor's front yard, observing the snow glistening in the moonlight. In front of a tree, she could see a few brave crocuses poking brightly colored blooms from out of the drifts of snow--a sign that spring was just around the corner. "I must make some changes," she resigned to herself. "I'm going to sell the house and get a small place; something that Len's insurance will cover until I can find employment during the evening hours. That way I can school the girls during the day and Mom can be with them in the evening." She continued to scuff up snow, wondering what the manager of the bakery would say if she strode in and laid out her ultimatum. "If the bakery doesn't offer me an evening position, then I'll have to do something else. The girls mean too much to me."

Janice put the house on the real estate market that week, along with receiving evening hours at the bakery. She was relieved to find the proprietor of the bakery eager to keep her on as the cake decorator, and was eager to help her adjust the schedule to meet the needs of the family. When Katy called to invite the family for dinner, Janice forgot about the past confrontations and gladly came, bubbling over with details concerning her new job and the sale of the house.

"I wish I had room for you all here," Katy said. "I would love to have you and the girls live with us."

"That's sweet of you." Janice sighed. "I've decided to buy a townhouse or something. We really don't need this fancy house. The Realtor was certain the house would fetch a good price."

"Come over for dinner and we can talk about it."

Janice arrived with Mary and Lisa in tow to be greeted by the pleasing aroma of lasagna and Italian bread spread with garlic butter. The cousins immediately took the girls under their wing while Janice went into the kitchen to help with dinner preparations.

"It's so good to see you again," Katy said with a hug before her face disintegrated into a picture of pain. When they parted, Janice noted in alarm the contorted lines crisscrossing the thin, pale cheeks of Katy's face. She then saw the gaunt features of her fragile body outlined beneath the skirt and blouse.

"Is something wrong, Katy? You look thin."

"Oh no. Paul says I'm turning into an old lady. I think I might have arthritis or something."

"At your age?"

Katy turned to the sink to wash up a few dishes leftover from the lasagna that now baked inside the oven. "My mother had arthritis in both knees which eventually required knee replacements. I've noticed pain in my joints, so I guess it's hereditary. I've also been pretty tired."

"Maybe you should see the doctor."

Katy shook her head. "Not for simple arthritis. I put some cream on the joints at night and prop myself up on a pillow. I feel better in no time. I told Paul I guess I'm just not getting enough sleep."

Janice opened her mouth to say more when a hearty, masculine greeting filled the air. Paul sauntered in, dumping a large briefcase filled with English papers from school on the table. "Why, hello stranger!" he said to Janice.

"Hi, yourself."

He came and gave her a friendly hug before sweeping Katy into his arms. "And how is the most famous cook in the whole world?"

"Watch it, you're hurting my back again, Paul," Katy reprimanded with a tight smile. "You'd better be careful with those manly hugs of yours. Either you're getting stronger or I'm a wimp."

Paul released her and stepped back. "Sorry, I forgot. And you are no wimp, my dear. My bear hugs just ain't what they used to be." He then turned to Janice. "I'm sure Katy has already told you about her aches and pains. She's also been having a lot of nosebleeds and canker sores."

"I think she should get checked out. After what happened with Len, I can't stand the thought of someone refusing to see a doctor and waiting to get their ailment diagnosed before it's too late." Janice felt the tears swim in her eyes. She tried to stifle them, but they flowed down her cheeks all the same. "Sorry," she confessed, reaching for a box of tissues sitting on the counter. "I shouldn't be telling you what to do."

"I appreciate your concern," Katy told her with a smile. "It's only natural that you'd feel edgy after what's happened. I'll be all right. Likely I'm battling some kind of virus. The flu is going around the office where I work."

Janice watched Katy fish out the makings for a lettuce salad from the crisper inside the refrigerator. "Let me do that."

Katy surrendered the head of lettuce and package of tomatoes to Janice who went to work slicing and fixing the salad into a silver bowl. Janice noticed Paul standing nearby, watching her work. She could see an expression of concern emanating in his dark eyes and wrinkled brow. The face, so like Len's from days gone by, sent a shiver racing through her. She averted her gaze to the tomatoes on the cutting board.

"So is everything okay?" he asked.

"Why wouldn't it be?"

He shrugged. "I don't know. It's just Katy and I were worried about..." He paused. Janice glanced over at Katy to see a look materializing on her face, accompanied by a slight shake of her head. "Never mind."

Janice scraped the sliced tomatoes into the bowl. "If you're worried about my past actions, I can report that I'm much better now. I think I'm over the hump, so to speak. I've finally gotten rid of many of Len's things. I donated a lot of his medical books and equipment to the office where he once practiced."

Both Katy and Paul looked at her. "I'm sure that was hard," Katy said softly.

"Yes, but it needed to be done. I know he isn't coming back, no matter how much I want him to. I have to go on with life. That's why I think moving out of the house will be the best thing for us. There are too many memories there. Of course there are plenty more items to be sold or given away. Now that I mention it, Paul, if you or the boys want Len's tablet, you're welcome to it."

"Now Jan, you don't need to..." he began.

"I don't really care about it. Dan and Pat seem into electronic toys the last time we talked. I use my cell phone, so I don't need it. It's one less thing I need to worry about, especially with a move." *And one less memory*, she added silently.

Both Katy and Paul continued to stare at her. Janice heaved a sigh, hoping they weren't trying to psychoanalyze her generosity. She only felt an increasing urge to wipe clean the slate filled with painful memories. Despite the new image she tried desperately to muster before the family, the dinner table remained subdued. The cousins jabbered away with each other, but Katy and Paul said little. Janice felt confused and uncomfortable. Perhaps they were still angry with her over the hostile encounters of the past. Janice stabbed a bit of lasagna on her fork and thrust it down her throat. The evening remained quiet until Paul and Katy sat with her inside the comfortable surroundings of the family room.

"Janice," Katy began, "we're glad you're trying to get your life back together, but we're still concerned about a few things."

Janice glanced between Paul and Katy. She felt a warmth rise in her cheeks. "This looks like an inquisition."

"It's not. We just care about you. For one thing, we were curious to know when you might be coming back to church. The pastor asked us last Sunday, as well as several members of the congregation. You know it's been over a year. That's a long time to be on your own without a church family."

Janice traced a pathway across a thin colored stripe that crisscrossed the fabric of her shirt. "I'm still trying to work that part out."

"Are you angry with God about what happened to Len?"

The question hovered in the air like a bomb waiting to drop. Janice put on her best smile while trying to duck the convicting question launched in her direction. "No. I...well, I might go to church somewhere else. It depends on where we end up once the house is sold." She laughed a little, fighting to conceal the pain bubbling up inside. "It's like life you know. You never know where it's going to lead you. I never thought I'd be a widow until I was at least eighty."

Silence prevailed in the room while Janice watched their reactions. Paul bobbed his knees back and forth. Katy continued to stare in sympathy, seeking to help wherever she could.

"Jan, you know that God loves you so much. He wants to be close to you in your time of need. He doesn't want you to bear all this alone."

"Unfortunately I am bearing it alone, and I think I'm doing a pretty good job."

"You know that's not true. Anyone can see how you're putting up a brave front, but quite frankly, you're dying inside."

Janice inhaled a sharp breath as the words stabbed her heart. *Dying! Dying like Len?* "How can you say that? I would think you'd be happy that I'm finally getting my act together, and I haven't collapsed from a nervous breakdown. I have a job that I absolutely love, the girls seem much happier now that I can spend days with them, and I'm taking steps toward securing our future. Now you say that I'm dying?"

"You're doing it all without God." Katy leaned forward in earnestness. "Jan, without God you won't survive in this world. You can try to survive by covering up your pain with all these decisions. But what's left once the decisions are finished? What do you have to live for? Your girls? Will your girls find true happiness and love if they know their mother has forsaken God at a time when you all needed Him the most?"

The agony of the words became unbearable. Janice jumped to her feet. "I don't care to hear any more of this." She swiped up her purse from off the ground. "If I had known you were going to do this to me, I would have never come."

"Jan, please," Katy pleaded. "We care so much about you, but God cares more."

"If God cares so much about me, why did He take Len away and leave me all alone to fend for myself? Huh? Do you have a pat answer for that one too?" Janice wiped the tears from her face before calling for her girls.

"Jan, don't leave like this," Paul intervened. "You can't think when you're upset. Let's just sit and talk this out. Katy and I only want to help."

"I can think just fine, and I can also make my own decisions without others making them for me." She hustled both Mary and Lisa out the door while asking her what was wrong. Janice glanced back once to see the sorrowful faces of the family staring at her from between the parted curtains. She wished her heart was strong enough to accept their love, but it remained imprisoned by a painful past.

Chapter 10

Janice continued on with life as best she could, schooling the girls during the day and working evenings at the bakery. Her relationship with her mother improved with Lucinda doggedly assisting in the girls' schooling and smiling for the first time when the girls performed their work to her satisfaction. Potential buyers cruised around the house with their realtors, but no offers came. Winter turned to spring, and then to summer. For a small vacation, Janice packed up the car and took the girls to the beach where they spent time enjoying the sun and sand. Watching them romp in the warm ocean waters, she could not help recalling Len's offer of a beach vacation during happier times within the family. Now there was nothing but emptiness and his words that seemed to fade with the passage of time. Katy's observation was coming true. She felt as if she was slowly dying. At home her eyes would dart to the devotional books and the Bible she used to read with all her heart until cancer devastated her marriage. Now the books collected layers of dust beneath the lamp stands where she had placed them. Occasionally she recalled Katy's heartfelt plea for her to reconsider attending church. The pastor called several times, asking her to return. Janice politely declined his invitation, telling him she was undecided about church. She considered her life up until that point. Nothing seemed to go right with God in the picture. "Maybe I was foolish to believe in it all," she said aloud. "I believed in Him and He only brought me pain." She laid down the brush to consider the statement. "Yet nothing seems right without Him."

One afternoon during a shopping trip, Janice stopped by the bakery to pick up a loaf of crusty French bread to go along with the meal planned for that evening. With the bag in one arm, she proceeded down the sidewalk, past the window of the coffee shop, when she noticed a man hunched over a cup in a corner table of the establishment. She paused in her walk and stared at the familiar form. Memories of Len swept over her as she observed the dark wavy hair sprinkled with gray, and a tawny colored hand clasping a coffee cup. Len always enjoyed coffee and loved coming to a place that brewed gourmet blends. She blinked, watching the scene change as she materialized on the other end of the table, laughing and talking while Len's hand reached out to grasp her hand in a loving hold. Without thinking, Janice walked into the coffee shop to find Paul sitting alone at the table. He took out a handkerchief to blow his nose before stuffing it into his pants pocket and returning to his coffee.

Inhaling a breath, Janice walked over and sat down opposite him, placing her bag on the floor. "Hi, Paul."

He jerked his head up in surprise. "Jan!"

"I was walking by the shop and saw a familiar face. For a moment I thought Len had come back to visit me. How I wish." She laughed softly, trying to conjure up a chuckle from the solemn figure.

His lips curved into a weak smile before focusing his attention on his coffee.

"Uh...how are you?"

"I've been better."

"Is something wrong?"

He took a sip of the steaming brew before setting it down again on the table. "Yeah, there is. We didn't want to tell you...not yet anyway."

Janice felt the temperature rise within her, and her heart take off in a foot race. "Tell me what?"

Paul blew out a sigh. "It's Katy. She's...well, she's pretty sick."

Janice straightened in her seat. Tension filled every muscle. "What's the matter with her?"

Paul struggled for the words before reaching for his handkerchief again. "She'd been losing all this weight in recent weeks, and the nosebleeds have been on the rise. I got worried, but you know her. She just waved it off and went on her merry way. She's so full of life, much more than I'll ever be. Then one evening she passed out on the bathroom floor. The boys and I, we managed to get her to bed before I called 911." His head slumped to his chest, his voice cracking as he spoke. "They drew blood to find out what was wrong. Jan, she's got acute leukemia."

Leukemia. The word struck Janice like the blow of a bat. She reeled and pushed her chair back from the table. "Leukemia. No, not Katy. That can't be."

"I don't know what I'm going to do." The choking gave way to tears that dribbled down his prickly cheeks. "The doctors say it's widespread in her system, like a plague. It's like some nightmare. I don't understand it. She's been in the hospital now for ten days, having extensive Chemotherapy to try and control it. If they can't get her white count under control, they say she might not make it."

The words chilled Janice like ice-cold water thrown on her flesh. Her lower lip began to tremble. Goosebumps emerged on her skin. "Paul, why didn't you tell me?"

"Katy didn't want me to. She said you'd been through enough with Len. I thought about it many times, but I know you've been pretty busy."

"I'm not so busy that I can't help. You were there when I needed you. I want to be there for you."

"I appreciate that." He blew his nose again before confessing, "I feel like a sissy, crying like this. I try not to lose it in front of the boys. They want a tough dad to keep them together, you know. Guess that's why I come here - to let it all out. I'm getting to be a regular in this place. I always sit in the same spot, here in this corner. I'm surprised they haven't engraved my name in the seat." He lifted the cup to his face, staring at the black liquid tainted with sugar and cream. "And to think when I was younger I couldn't stand the taste of coffee. Guess everything in life changes."

"Don't worry about the crying, Paul. You wouldn't be human if you didn't cry. I used to complain to a friend of mine about the boxes of tissues I went through during Len's illness. It's normal, even for men."

Paul's watery eyes met hers. "Guess you would understand this better than anyone, wouldn't you?"

Janice nodded. "Even Jesus wept. It's the shortest verse of the Bible." Scriptures of comfort that she had not entertained since Len's death filled her mind. At that moment she realized her preoccupation with her own grief. The darkness of it all had been like an idol, shutting her away from the light and comfort she might have found in God's word. She desperately wanted Paul to find comfort during this time of upheaval, yet the mere idea of sharing Scripture when she herself had not lived the words seemed hypocritical. "Are the kids okay?"

"I guess so. Karen is taking it pretty hard. Dan...well, he seems to be the strongest of the three. He's involved in some kind of prayer group at school. You've heard about those groups that meet around the flagpole? He does that and it seems to help him cope." Paul downed the rest of his coffee. "It's weird, but I think I understand a little of what you were trying to tell us a few months ago...about not understanding God's purpose in all of this. I sure don't understand why this is happening, especially to a woman like Katy. She's so strong and beautiful and godly. She...she doesn't deserve to suffer like this." He bent his head, shielding his face from Janice's view, even as she watched a teardrop leave a tiny glistening puddle on the wooden surface of the table.

Janice sighed. "I guess that's the biggest struggle of all - when things don't go the way we planned. We think we have life all sorted out, wrapped up in neat packages, ready to open when we want. We get to the point when we're finally ready to open the big daddy, and instead of a nice gift, we receive something rotten to the core. But there has to be something good come of it." She bent her head, realizing she had not considered the goodness to be found in Len's passing. She had only complained, argued, and prayed he would rise up out of the grave and come home. Len's passing had stirred up an internal strength and understanding that she could now pass on to others.

"You wouldn't believe how strong Katy's been through all this," Paul confessed, blowing his nose for the fourth time into his soggy handkerchief. "I mean, she just lays there with tubes running out of her, quoting the Bible and telling me how everything works out for the good. I'm trying hard to stand with her, but I feel weak compared to her. And she's the one sick as a puppy." He chuckled in scorn. "I used to think I was such a tough guy, too. Guess I thought I had to be tough to handle a bunch of high school students who'd rather be anywhere than in my English class. But when things like this happen, I just fall apart."

Janice nodded, realizing all too well the pain of questions, indecision, and sorting through the answers if there were any to be found. She could not help but marvel at the similarities between Paul's pain and her own.

"I'd better get on over to the hospital," he announced, rising to his feet. He scratched his head of salt and pepper colored hair as he picked up the empty coffee cup. "Look at that - I didn't even offer to buy you a cup of coffee. I guess I am losing it."

"Don't worry about it."

"Do you want to see Katy?"

Janice rose instantly to her feet. "Oh, do you think it would be all right? I mean, you said she didn't want me to know."

"You know now, so you might as well see her. Like you said, we need family standing with each other at a time like this."

"I'm parked down the street. I'll follow you to the hospital."

Paul nodded as he held the door of the shop open for her. Janice heaved a sigh as she threw her own bundle into the back seat of the car and fumbled with nervous fingers to push the key into the ignition. The mere thought of seeing another loved one suffering in the cancer unit of the University Hospital conjured up painful memories. On the way to the familiar sight of the huge white building and adjacent parking garage, she recalled Len in his last days, sitting listlessly in a huge cushioned chair, his feet swollen to three times their normal size, his yellow face and eyes gazing dolefully at her. Janice winked back the tears. Her fingers gripped the steering wheel of the car. "God, I don't know if I can go through this again," she whispered. "I just don't have the strength. I know I've talked about how strong I am - finding the job, putting the house on the market, keeping the family in order. But the truth is, my strength has to come from You." She slowed and turned into the parking garage. "I'm sorry I've been doing this in my own strength. Help me find Your strength in this time of need." As she rolled into a parking space next to Paul's van, a sensation of peace filled her unlike anything she had experienced in months. Despite the memories that wrestled against the newfound strength, she walked with confidence into the massive hospital and into the elevators that would whisk her to Katy's bedside.

The odor permeating the cancer unit was just as Janice remembered - the sickly sweet odor of disease infecting humanity. Sometimes Janice would recognize the same cancerous odor on Len before she doused him with aftershave to mask the smell. Drawing a deep breath to steady herself, she walked bravely beside Paul into the private room where a woman lay in bed, staring out the window at the bright sunshine and the birds flying in mid-air.

Katy turned her head. Her pale face with large eyes surrounded by dark circles stared as she looked first at Janice, then at Paul. Her thin lips, cracked and bleeding, opened to reveal sores dotting the interior of her mouth. Janice winced and bit down on her own lip.

"I had to tell her, Katy," Paul said, stooping to give his wife a kiss. "She found me at my old stomping ground - the coffee shop."

"It's just as well." Katy held out her hand, which Janice grasped. The hand felt bony and cold, despite the mass of blankets covering Katy's emaciated form. "I'm so glad you're here."

"I am, too," Janice said, "but not in this place." She turned away, trying hard not to let Katy see her tears.

"It must be difficult coming to the same unit where Len passed away." Katy leaned back against her pillow and sighed. "But I often think about what he experienced on that day, lying in his bed, ready to enter eternity. Just think, he saw the majesty of heaven. He saw that light at the end of the tunnel so many talk about, which we know is the light of Christ." Her pale, thin lips curved into a smile. "Just think that Jesus came to visit him here, in a place like this. The God of heaven and earth visited His beloved child. He wrapped his arms around Len and took him home. Isn't that the most amazing thing?"

Janice fumbled with the strap to her purse while Paul paced back and forth before the hospital window, watching buses and cars honk their horns at each other from the street below. Finally he turned and glared at Katy. "How come every time I visit, you talk about dying? Why can't you talk about fighting this?"

The harsh tone of his voice sent both Katy and Janice staring at him in stunned surprise.

Katy struggled to sit up in the bed. "Honey, don't you know why? One day with the Lord is better than a thousand days here."

"Away from your family? Away from those who love you? Now it's time to give up?"

"I'm not giving up, but I'm not holding back either. I'll let God decide what He wants to do with me. I know He can heal me, but I also know He can heal me forever by taking me home to be with Him."

"Terrific. God would want a mother and wife to go and be with Him when we need her here. If that's the kind of God you serve, count me out." Paul strode out of the room.

"I'm sorry about Paul," Katy said softly. "Please, Jan, sit down here with me."

Janice slowly drew up a chair and sat down, averting her eyes from the clicking machine at the bedside dripping fluids into Katy's arm, and the oxygen set-up on the wall behind the bed.

"Paul is getting more and more agitated about my condition." Katy sighed. "I pray for him all the time. Maybe you can help him understand, Jan."

Janice opened her mouth to respond, but no words would come out.

"I need you to reach him, to reach my family." Katy groped for her hand once more. "I've thought a lot about what you went through. I know you endured it just for this time, Jan."

Janice nodded. "I came to that conclusion on the way here. Paul's anger is similar to Len's in many respects."

"You weren't angry when Len was diagnosed with his cancer?"

"More confused, I guess. I know he needed me and so did the girls. I tried to stay strong and never let him see my feelings. But I know there were many times I cried myself to sleep."

Katy nodded. "Paul and I...we're inseparable. Everyone knew we were meant for each other the moment we met. That's why I'm so afraid for him...for our family...for the future."

"Katy, you mustn't think you won't recover. The Bible says that God heals our diseases."

"I know. I've had the pastor and the elders anoint me and ask for healing. But you know that sometimes God heals in mysterious ways."

"A friend once told me that," Janice admitted, recalling the day of the fateful blizzard and her conversation with one of her customers named Cindy. "She told me how God sometimes performs an everlasting healing by taking the loved one away from the pain and the confusion of life. But you're young, Katy. You have a husband and children who love you. Don't give up."

"Oh dear Jan," Katy said softly, squeezing her hand. "I-I must tell you something. Please, don't tell Paul, not yet. It would break his heart if he found out. The doctor was here this morning. He told me the Chemotherapy isn't working at all like he expected. The abnormal cells are multiplying so rapidly, that can't control it. I-I'll need a miracle."

Janice sucked in her breath. The tears swam in her eyes like so many shed in the face of cancer. The image of the sickly woman lying in bed wavered before her like an image reflecting on water. "Oh Katy, this can't be happening. There must be something they can do."

"I wish there was. They discussed a bone marrow transplant, but I'm so weak right now that my system would probably reject it. With God there is hope, but I know He's been speaking to my heart, getting me ready for whatever lies ahead. There are others who need to get ready, like my children and Paul. I know God has brought you here to be a special part in my family's lives in the days ahead." The hand slipped away. Katy's eyelids grew heavy from fatigue.

"You're tired," Janice said softly, brushing back a strand of soft brown hair that had fallen across Katy's face. "Don't you worry about anything. I will help you and your family."

Katy smiled once more. "I know you will, Jan."

Janice slipped a quick kiss on her cheek before venturing out into the hallway, looking around for the familiar form of Paul. She finally found him in the visitor's lounge with another cup of coffee in his hand. He never glanced in her direction as he sipped the beverage. Instead he stared hollowly out the window that overlooked the parking garage.

"You probably think I'm an awful husband," he muttered. "You think I should be more understanding."

"I think you're trying to understand," Janice said softly. She came and stood by his side, sharing in the view. "It takes time."

"I just don't understand her. All she talks about is how wonderful heaven's going to be. It's like she's given up the ship. How can she do that? How can she just give up?"

"She isn't giving up. It's just a process the dying go through."

"The dying?" His eyes glared at Janice with an intensity that sent her gaze shifting to a plotted plant in the corner of the room. "So that's it? You've given up hope, too?"

Janice remained silent, pondering her response. Finally she said, "Paul, I held on to hope for Len's recovery until the last possible moment. He was the one who told me there was no hope for him in this world. I realized then that he had hope in another place, a better place, one that we can't even begin to imagine while we live here on earth. I know it's taken me all this time to come to grips with Len's death, but I think I understand now what he was trying to say, and perhaps what Katy is saying, too. Despite the fact we love them and want them with us, there really is a much better place than this world. And if we really love them, we know that place is where they should be, without pain or hardship, safe with God."

"Well, I won't pretend to understand. The kids need Katy. I need Katy. I..." He paused. A cry rose up in his throat, which he muffled with his shirtsleeve. "Oh God, this pain is too much. You can't take her from me. You just can't. How will I live?" He threw the cup in the trash and walked out.

Janice sunk her head into her hands and prayed fervently for the first time in many long months.

Chapter 11

Janice never would have imagined a harder funeral than the one she endured after Len's death, yet Katy Dawson's funeral surpassed it. Unlike her own reaction at Len's funeral where she stood like a chiseled statue, going through the motions of greeting guests, Paul displayed a strange euphoria that Janice could not understand. During the funeral he joked around with the visitors, played ball with the kids while the guests ate dinner, and laughed in such a way as to leave Janice with a sensation like bugs crawling along her skin. Sitting quietly by herself, watching his reactions from afar, Janice knew the turmoil he must be suffering. She knew the laughter and the jokes were all fronts to hide what lurked within him.

In the weeks that followed, thoughts of Paul and his family consumed her. Numerous times she tried calling the house, only to find Paul out and the kids left alone to fend for themselves. Several afternoons she came by with a plate of cookies or freshly baked brownies to find herself inundated by the children's loneliness. Karen latched onto her as if she were her mother. Dan and Pat remained reserved, but would occasionally talk to Janice about their schoolwork or the sports teams they were involved in. Paul's stark absence loomed over the house. Occasionally Janice would go by the coffee shop on her way to the bakery to find Paul sitting in his usual spot, sipping coffee and talking with himself. Sometimes he wrote furiously on a legal pad. Other times he only stared out into space. Janice tried having conversations with him on numerous occasions, but he would climb to his feet in a hurry, claiming some engagement.

Finally Janice cornered Paul in a grocery store while he was buying food and begged him to accept a dinner invitation. Now she bustled about the large kitchen in her home that had not yet sold, fixing an Italian feast of chicken cacciatore and spaghetti. Her mother had left the week before to pay her bills and check on her apartment, leaving Janice to look after the girls and put them off on the neighbors while she went to work. As she fixed a salad, she wondered if Paul could care for the girls a few evenings a week until her mother arrived back. The girls would feel better having friendly playmates, and it might prompt him to stay at home where he was needed.

An hour before the family was due to arrive, Janice hurried into the bedroom to throw on some nice clothes. She even put on make-up and gardenia perfume from a new bottle. For a moment she stared at her reflection in the mirror, examining the thin line of her cheekbones, green eyes, lips tainted with red lipstick, and wavy brown hair dancing around her shoulders. She wondered if she was still an attractive woman, despite all that she had gone through.

When the doorbell rang, a pang of apprehension nipped her. Karen rushed into the home, delivering Janice a hug before seeking out Mary and Lisa to play Barbie dolls in their room. Dan and Pat casually walked in with their hands thrust into the pockets of baggy jeans, looking around the home. Behind them came Paul, wearing a dirty sweatshirt and stained sweat pants, appearing as if he had just come from exercising somewhere in the great outdoors. The smell of perspiration lingered in the air.

"Here we are," he exclaimed.

"Glad you could make it," Janice said, trying not to let his disheveled appearance ruffle her. She flushed a bit when he sniffed the perfume in the air, then centered his eyes on her for a moment. His mouth opened, ready to issue some remark, before shutting it tight.

"You look like you could use something to drink," she said hastily, retreating to the kitchen.

"A coke would be great." Paul flopped down on the couch, with the boys taking seats nearby. They sat stiff and silent while Janice hurriedly poured the drinks.

"Thanks," Paul said as he gulped down the beverage. "That hits the spot."

Janice stood awkwardly in the room, wondering what to say. They all seemed like strangers to her rather than family. The boys appeared like sheep lost in a wilderness of confusion, while their father lived in a strange world that no one could access.

"So how is school going, boys?" Janice finally asked.

"Oh fine," Pat said carelessly, fiddling with the shoelace to his sneaker.

"Pretty good," Dan echoed.

"Are you still part of that prayer group at school, Dan?" Janice watched the eyes of both Pat and Paul focused on the boy with an intensity she did not understand.

Dan squirmed uncomfortably. "Yeah, I joined the one they've got now in the new school we're going to. You know we're going to Middleview instead of Parkside Christian School."

Janice nodded. *The public school where Paul teaches. I guess they had to since Katy passed away. Her job helped support a private institution.* "That's good you've found another group. I often wished I had a group like that back when I was in high school. It can get pretty hard at times, with the peer pressure and the work. I'll bet you like seeing your dad in the hallway though, huh Pat?"

Pat squirmed and continued to examine his sneakers. Paul said nothing.

Janice exhaled a long sigh before returning to the kitchen. "Dinner will be ready in just a few minutes," she called. Inside the kitchen, she leaned over the counter and nearly broke down in frustration. Clearly the little family was hurting, but what could she do? She felt spiritually weak herself, unable to bear the burden of their pain. Janice had only recently returned to church to find open acceptance among the congregation and the pastor. However the renewal of her spiritual life did not strengthen her in time to face the onslaught of depression and confusion circulating within Paul's family.

Janice pushed the thoughts aside to concentrate on completing the dinner preparations. She set the table with her second best dinnerware and a flowered centerpiece. When the girls bounded out, they oohed and ahhed over the pretty flowers. The men said nothing but took their seats and waited politely for the prayer.

Janice placed her napkin on her lap and looked up expectantly at Paul who now began downing the ice water placed before him. "Paul, would you like to offer the blessing?"

He set down the water glass with a thump. Droplets clung to his grizzled chin from day old beard stubble. "I think you should since you're the lady of the house."

Janice shrugged. She bent her head and offered a simple prayer of thanks for the food and the family. She then began passing the dishes. The family ate little, including Paul who only drank copious amounts of water. After finishing his own drink, he proceeded to empty Karen's glass. Shaking her head, Janice rose to fill a glass pitcher with ice water and place it before him.

"If you're going to drink the reservoir, I might as well supply you with it."

Paul glanced up in surprise. The children broke out into gales of laughter that eased the tension in the room. "Guess I have drank my fair share," he observed.

"More than that. I hope you don't float away."

He shrugged and poured another helping. "I've been working out at the rec center in town," he confessed. "Brings out the sweat in you."

"So that's where you've been hiding. I've visited the kids a couple of times, but I never find you around."

"They can take care of themselves. They're plenty old enough. Besides, exercise is good for the soul."

"But is it good for the family?" Janice asked before wishing she could take back the comment.

Anger broke out like hives across Paul's face. "Just what is that supposed to mean?" he barked.

"I didn't mean anything," Janice said quietly.

"I suppose you're going to tell me that I should spend every waking moment with my kids. Yeah, I hear that all over. Well, I do, don't I?" He glared around the table. The tone sent the children sliding down in their seats and eyes staring at their plates of food.

"Let's not worry about it. How about some more garlic bread, Dan?" She passed the plate to the boy, ignoring the look on Paul's face. Dinner remained subdued for the rest of the evening. After dessert the girls scurried off to the bedroom while the boys investigated the dartboard located in the basement. Janice immediately took up the task of the dishes, ignoring Paul who stood in the doorway with his arms folded across his chest.

"So what did you mean by that comment at dinner?"

His deep voice sent her whirling about in a start. For an instant she saw Len standing there, demanding an answer to his question. She shook her head and returned to stacking the dishes inside the dishwasher.

"So now you won't tell me. Isn't that just typical of a woman. Evelyn cornered me the other day at school, laying it out about my teaching style, and then refusing to go into detail. Nosy busybodies."

"Paul, I'm just concerned about your kids," Janice said softly as she slid in plates between the plastic prongs. "They need you so much right now, especially after losing their mother."

"I can't nursemaid them twenty-four hours a day. I'm not a mother hen."

"I know that, but when I saw my girls turning into introverts, I realized I had to make changes. That's why I moved my job to evenings so I could spend time with them. It's really helped."

He laughed scornfully. "Well there's no teaching jobs at night unless I teach college courses. I don't happen to have that kind of degree."

Janice began stacking the glasses one by one. "That's not what I mean. Take this exercise that you do every evening. Maybe you can take the kids with you. I'm sure they'd have lots of fun. I just don't know if it's good for them to be alone so much after losing their mother." She inhaled a breath. "And I wanted to ask if it might be possible to keep Lisa and Mary a few times a week while I work evenings. I know Karen would enjoy their company. Then if you need to go out a night or two on your own, I'll look after your kids."

"I see you have our lives all mapped out."

"No...but like you and Katy once told me, we have to go on with our lives the best way we know how."

"Well Katy isn't here anymore, so now you have to deal with me. And I'm telling you right now to mind your own business and I'll mind mine." He turned and ventured down to the basement to gather up his boys.

Janice watched the children herded out the door, not unlike what she had done the night Katy and Paul tried to reach her hard heart. She could not help but marvel at the similarities between herself and Paul. Both of them were stubborn people who had lost their companions and were now trying to cope in the midst of horrific pain and confusion. Could there really be a hidden purpose in all of this?

At the bakery later that week, Janice busied herself with putting the finishing touches on a cake she had prepared for a Bon Voyage party. The cake, in the shape of a globe with the seven continents neatly outlined in dark frosting, stood out in sharp contrast with the tinted baby blue frosting to simulate the ocean waters. Janice smiled when she looked at it until an enthusiastic voice greeted her.

"You still have the decorator's touch. That cake is simply gorgeous!"

Janice turned to see a familiar face from a long ago, but she couldn't place it. The woman held out her hand. "Remember me, Cindy? You drove through a blizzard to deliver me a Yule log cake on time for a Christmas party?"

"Oh Cindy, how could I forget you," Janice breathed. She wiped the frosting from her hands on a towel before shaking the hand Cindy offered.

"I tried calling you several times, but there was no answer. I see now where you ended up. I must say it's right up your alley."

"I work evenings now. That way I can home-school the girls during the day."

"The cake is beautiful," Cindy acknowledged once more. "How are you doing these days?"

"Much better." Janice pulled up a chair for her to sit. "I spent a good year mourning for Len until God woke me up. It was a rude awakening, though. Len's sister-in-law contracted leukemia suddenly."

"Oh, how terrible."

"Yes, and she died six weeks later. We were all stunned. The cancer had spread so rapidly, the chemotherapy just didn't have time to work."

Cindy's hand encompassed hers in a firm hold. "I'm so sorry. Two partings in one family...that is so difficult."

"I'm doing okay, but I'm concerned about my husband's brother, Paul. He seems to be going through the same stages that I went through. Of course he acts differently, but there are similarities in the anger and the depression. Sometimes it's mixed at times with an unnatural giddiness, like he's drunk or something. During Katy's funeral, he acted in the strangest way. He never mourned. In fact, I never saw him cry. He joked around and played games with the kids."

"His coping mechanism at the time," Cindy suggested.

"That's what I assumed, but it was unnerving to watch. And the kids - I feel so sorry for the kids. He has three children which he leaves alone most of the time so he can work out at the rec center or drink coffee at the downtown coffee shop."

"Hmm." Cindy fiddled with a napkin lying on the counter. "Have you tried talking to him?"

"He's like a brick wall right now. We had a family dinner a few weeks ago and it was a disaster. I guess I didn't give him enough time before I started giving him my opinion. I mean Katy's only been gone a few months. The kids need the attention so badly while Paul just wants to be by himself. Little Karen clings to me whenever I visit. I know I need to stay in contact with the family, even if Paul hates me for voicing my opinion. The kids need the love of a parent right now."

"Oh, I don't think he hates you. I'm sure he hates what has happened. Men are like that in most instances. They like to dominate a situation. Look at it from his point of view. The cancer took his wife away. The disease was the victor in his eyes, so to speak. He had no victory over it. He feels a loss, not only for his wife, but of his own self esteem."

"I wish there was some way to make him see things differently."

"You really can't tell a man what to do, Janice. I know you found that out with your husband. You can't be bullied by them, but you can't control them either. You need to support Paul and allow him to discover what's wrong in his own time."

Janice brightened at this suggestion. "I think I know what you mean. Once when Len was upset, I just listened to him and his interests. That's when he broke down and confessed what was inside."

Cindy spread open her hands. "There's your answer. Instead of telling Paul what to do, which he will resist, try to support him and the family. Do things for them, but be a listening ear. Let him come forth with his own answer and you'll be pleasantly surprised."

Her heart began to beat with excitement. "Yes, that's just what I'll do. It worked with Len, it must also work with Paul. After all, they are related. Oh Cindy, you're a lifesaver!"

"Which flavor?" she joked. "That was a horrible pun, wasn't it? One of my children picked that up from a friend. I laughed so hard I almost got sick. Oh well. Life should be fun. It does have painful moments, but God says the joy of the Lord is our strength." She rose to her feet.

Janice jumped up and gave her a hug. She felt energized by the conversation. "You're always there when I need you. Are you sure you're not an angel in disguise?"

Cindy laughed. "I guess we never know sometimes. Take care, Janice. I'll be praying for you and the situation."

Janice turned back to her creation and picked up the pastry tube, ready to finish outlining the small countries comprising the continent of Europe. "That's just what I'm gonna do," she murmured aloud, watching the continent unfold along the outline she had created in the blue frosting. "I won't let Paul off the hook."

Chapter 12

Paul tried whistling a tune as he parked the car in a space near the community recreation center, but he felt no joy as he had in past months before his life turned upside down. For the last several weeks he considered what Jan had told him concerning his kids. The other day he took the kids to a movie, along with treating them to popcorn and drinks, but a strange moodiness had overshadowed them. The boys rarely discussed what was happening in their lives. Karen willingly gave of herself as little girls usually did, but Paul sensed a distance forming between the kids and himself that he did not understand. The mere thought of losing control over his family sent his fist slamming with frustration into the steering wheel. "Why did you have to leave me like this, Katy?" he groaned. "You were the one who kept the house under control. You kept the kids in a private school, which they really liked. You made us feel happy. Now it's all going down the tubes and I can't stop it."

Paul regretted putting the kids back into the public school, but after Katy's death, there was little money to continue funding a private education. He tried to make the best of the situation. Pat ignored him in the hallway at school when Paul would give him a thumbs up. Dan continued to be the thoughtful, pious one in the family. He often read his Bible - an act that convicted Paul, much to his dismay. Occasionally Paul took Karen to the playground down the street. Sometimes he tossed baseballs to the boys. Yet the children would not confide in him as they had in the past. Paul glanced up at the reinforced concrete building of the athletic center, wondering if he should take up Jan's suggestion and invite the boys to participate in an exercise regimen. He needed a breakthrough before he lost everything.

Paul picked up his black duffel bag and walked inside. The sights and sounds of the gym were all around - the clanging of weights, the voices of personal trainers teaching their students the ins and outs of shaping up, the faint music serenading an aerobics class. Paul showed his pass and immediately headed for the lockers, stuffing the bag in the usual place. He then bent to re-tie his sneakers with firm tugs on the laces. *Should I quit doing this?* he wondered. *Am I being insensitive to the kids' needs? No, I can't quit. I need this place. If I don't come here and lift the weights, I can't release the frustration inside me. I'll go crazy, maybe even take out my frustration on the kids. No, I have to do this.* With determined strides he headed for the weight room where he heard the panting of others lifting weights. The odor of sweat permeated the room.

Finding the bench press open, he placed the pin at the desired weight and began to press rapidly. The exercise slowly relieved the tension in his muscles. Each time he lifted the weights, he felt the pain of Katy's death diminish; the forlorn appearances on his kids' faces disappear, and the harsh words of fellow teachers during the school day evaporate. Up and down, up and down. He began to huff with each press. Finally after two rounds of ten presses, he sat up. Trickles of perspiration cascaded down his neck and shoulders. His fingers groped for a towel on the floor until he realized he had forgotten to pick one up on his way out of the locker room. Paul swung his legs away from the press and stood up to see a young woman enter the weight room, dressed in exercise clothing that outlined her trim figure. Chestnut brown hair lay caught up in a ponytail. She appeared hesitant, glancing around with a strange expression as if trying to decide whether she was in the right place or not. The look on her face reminded him of someone, but he could not place it. Perhaps a fellow teacher from school. He shook his head and ventured to the lockers where the fresh towels were stacked. Rubbing his head into one, the tension within him began to return. Again he marched back to the weight room to use the leg press, only to find the young woman at one of the presses, gingerly lifting the lowest weight up and down with slow movements of her sleek legs. She glanced up, smiled brightly, and said, "This is good exercise, isn't it?"

He stared in disbelief. "Jan? What in the world are you doing here?"

"Getting in shape, I hope," she puffed before allowing the weight to sink down with a decisive clang. "That's enough for me." She whisked a towel up and wiped her sweaty face. "So this is what you do?"

"Yes, this is what I do. I thought you were against it the last time we talked." He sat down hard on the press next to her, adjusted the weight, and began to pump. With each stroke of the press he observed the muscles tighten into firm ripples along his thighs.

Jan stood silently, watching him. "Len used to lift weights when we first met," she commented. "After we were married, he got too busy with his practice to keep up with it."

Paul continued to press rapidly until the sweat again built up on his face and trickled down his back. Finally he allowed the weight to drop with a decisive thump.

"Have you tried the pool yet?" Jan asked. "I love to swim. I took the girls to the beach this summer, but of course you can't do much swimming in the ocean. The pool here looks terrific."

"I don't swim. I usually lift weights."

"Well if you want to join me, I'm going to take a swim. See you." She wrapped the towel around her neck, waved cheerfully, and made off for the lockers. Paul sat on the bench and shook his head, wondering what spawned the sudden change of interest within her. He pondered the idea of continuing his usual regimen inside the weight room, but remembering her friendly invitation, decided to check out the pool. When he arrived after changing into a pair of trunks, Jan was already in the water, performing perfect strokes across the length of the pool. Her curved arms gracefully plunged into the water; her long, sleek legs fluttering as she propelled herself easily from side to side. When she emerged from the aqua blue waters, Paul applauded.

"And the Olympic swimmer, Janice Dawson, has just broken the world record in freestyle, ladies and gentlemen," he announced with a smile.

Jan's eyes flew open in surprise before she floated up and splashed water on his feet. "All right, let's see what you can do."

He knelt next to her by the poolside and whispered, "All I can do is the doggy paddle. Don't tell anyone."

"That's not true, I'm sure," she said, laughing. Suddenly her hand reached out and grabbed his arm, yanking him headfirst into the pool with a terrific splash.

He rose quickly to the surface, shaking the water from his face. "Hey, what's the big idea?"

"Payback for what you did during my skating lesson," she said with a laugh. "Remember? You snuck up behind me and started pushing me across the ice?"

He slapped a hand to his forehead. "Ah ha, so it's old fashioned revenge. I forgot about the skating. But that didn't turn out so terrible. We actually had fun." He delved into the water and came up floating on his back, shooting a stream of water out of his mouth like a whale. Jan broke out in laughter over his antic. He turned his head, grinned, then began a perfect backstroke to the far side of the pool.

"That's pretty good for an old man," Jan shouted.

"Yeah, well I'm not ready for the wheelchair just yet," he retorted, swimming up beside her where she stood in hip deep water, resting an arm along the edge of the pool. He could not help but stare at her, watching the way the water dripped down the curved line of her cheeks and the brightness in her green eyes as they perused his. Strands of dripping wet hair, caught up in a ponytail, flowed over one shoulder, sending a fine stream of water running down her bathing suit. He shook his head, and with a jerk, turned and headed back out into the water. He sensed the guilt rise up within him for dwelling on Jan's attractive features as she stood calmly by the poolside. Now he pounded the water with his arms, ignoring the comments she sent his way. He rose out of the pool on the opposite side, only to find her walking toward him with a towel.

"Thanks," he said shortly, taking the towel from her outstretched hand. "Look, I gotta get going."

"All right. I had fun, Paul. Maybe we can do it again?"

"Yeah," he said, turning for the locker room. Despite his best effort, he could not shake the picture of Jan from his mind. He wanted to think of Katy, but she was no longer there. He had no wife to occupy his thoughts now. But Jan? Not Jan. She was family, his sister-in-law. He changed quickly, stuffed the wet trunks into the bag, and hastened for the nearest exit, fearful he might run into her again. Once inside the car, he shut the door and rested his head against the steering wheel. "I'm sorry, Katy. I know you're not here, but I must keep thinking of you no matter how hard it hurts. I won't think of another woman, and the least of all, Jan."

Janice was pleased at how well the outing went, though confused by the brusqueness of their departure as if the meeting had somehow rattled Paul. She could not fathom what troubled him, unless the anger from the ill-fated dinner a while back had spilled over into the outing. Yet she was glad for the opportunity to clown around like a young woman again. The idea of acting young gave her a hope for the future. Many times she stood before the mirror, wondering if God would send another man into her life. Now that Len had been gone almost two years, such thoughts occasionally crossed her mind. Janice missed eating dinner out at a fancy restaurant, feeling arms nestled around her, or just sharing in a quiet evening before the fire, sipping a mug of hot cider and talking about the future. She was too young to remain alone like this for the rest of her life. When the thoughts drove her into depression, she would pour out her frustrations to the Lord.

Janice walked in the door of the home to find her mother standing there with the real estate agent. She placed her bag on a nearby table and shook the realtor's hand.

"It looks like a couple's going to buy the house, Janice," Lucinda informed her. "And they are willing to give us our asking price."

"Really." Janice felt her heart sink to her toes. The reality of the impending sale took her by surprise. Now everything in her life seemed to be on the verge of great change. She prayed for the strength to endure it.

"Yes, and they are prepared to offer your asking price, Mrs. Dawson," the realtor said.

"That's very generous."

"Of course the couple wish to occupy the house in thirty days if that's not too much trouble."

Thirty days! Janice gulped, looking over at her mother who only stood with a fixed expression on her face. "I guess that will have to do since they are offering full price. I'll need time to look around for something else."

"Fine. I took the liberty of drawing up the contract. Just initial the parts where I have starred them and sign your name."

Janice took the contract with shaky hands, partly from the contract resting in her hand, and partly from her damp hair that left her chilled to the bone.

"I'll be in touch tomorrow. Have a good evening."

"Thank you," she said as she flipped through the contract. "Well Mother, I guess this is it."

"This house is too big for you anyway, Janice."

"I know. It's the best thing we can do. With such an offer, maybe we can buy ourselves another place. I should have enough of a downpayment so the mortgage won't be too bad."

"On a baker's salary?" her mother said, lifting an eyebrow.

"I still have several more years left on Len's money. I think I can make it work."

"If you say so."

Janice lifted her eyes to acknowledge her mother - noting the same brown hair, thin cheekbones, and square nose she had inherited. The image sparked an idea she had toyed with for several months. Despite the temperament of her mother and her demeanor that severely tested her patience, Janice knew she might need her to make the adjustment work. Yet a part of her rebelled at the thought of being with her mother twenty-four hours a day.

With a sigh, Janice said, "Mother, I was wondering whether you'd consider moving in with us permanently. That way we can split the costs. You don't need your apartment. As it is, you're leasing it now while you stay here with me and the girls."

"Thank you for the offer, but I'll have to think about it, Janice. I know things have been going a little better between us." Lucinda then pointed to Janice's hair that hung in damp strings about her shoulders. "Why is your hair wet, for goodness sake? Where have you been, the hairdresser?"

"Oh, I went to the recreation center in town," Janice said, opening up her bag to pull out her wet suit. "I just got a week's trial membership to try out the facilities. It's the same place Paul's been going to. I'm hoping maybe I can help him out of his depression and back into life once again."

Lucinda's eyebrows raised in a disapproving manner. "Do you think that's wise, Janice, swimming with another man?"

Janice laughed uncomfortably. "Mother, Paul is hardly just another man. He happens to be Len's brother."

"And he also happens to be a widower, don't forget."

"Mother, honestly." Janice strode off to rinse out the chlorine from the dripping suit before hanging it on a clothes rack to dry. Her mother tracked her every move like a shadow as she headed for the basement and the laundry room

"Janice, I think it's improper."

Janice hung the suit on the rack. "Mother, I don't see any reason why I can't reach out to Paul when he's hurting. We're related."

"You're not related by blood," Lucinda was quick to point out, "but if you keep up with these secret rendezvous of yours, you may very well end up related."

Janice whirled, her face beet red. "Mother!" She watched Lucinda walk off, leaving her embarrassed at the mere thought. "Oh God, You know what I was trying to do! I don't want Paul to turn into a hermit and treat life as if it holds nothing for him. I care about him and his family. Katy pleaded with me to take care of them. Please, show me what to do."

In the days that followed, Janice scoured the housing market with her agent and traipsed through many homes with her children and mother in tow, looking for the perfect place. In every home she found something to her dissatisfaction. One had the wrong colored carpet, another the wrong wallpaper. The bedrooms were too small or the kitchen countertops too green. Lucinda complained that she shouldn't be so picky and find a place soon. Janice scanned the housing ads on the Internet but came up empty.

She thought of possibly renting, or even moving in with her mother at her apartment. As the days ticked down, Janice only found herself in a quandary over what to do. She needed help finding a solution, but whom could she trust? At times like this, she missed Len and the advice he offered. All the decision-making frazzled her nerves to the breaking point, not unlike the jolt of electrical currents passing through her.

With all the busyness inherent in the sale, Janice neglected to keep up with Paul and the family. She had not returned to the rec center since their meeting, nor had she even talked to the family. Now desperate for some advice to her housing situation, she picked up her cell phone.

"Hi Pat, this is your Aunt Jan. How are you?" She paused, listening to her nephew while examining her fingernails and the ragged cuticles. Perhaps one day she should treat herself to a manicure when her life normalized a bit more. "That's great. I'm sure your father is very proud you made the basketball team. By the way, is he around?" She listened as Pat's voice called for his father. There was some commotion in the background. Janice tensed, wondering what was afoot, until a husky voice came on the line.

"Hello?"

"Hi Paul. How are you?"

"Fine."

"I...uh," Janice paused, hunting for the words. In a single instant her mind went blank. She felt her insides tighten with anxiety. "H-How's your family?"

"Doing good. Pat made the basketball team."

"So I heard. You must be very proud."

"Proud as punch."

"Look, I...oh, that's right, now I remember...I wanted to know if you've heard of any houses for sale."

"Houses for sale," he repeated.

"Yes, you see, I have to move out in less than two weeks and I'm trying to find something quick. So far it's been a dead end."

"I really don't keep track of the housing market, Jan. I'm an English teacher not a Real Estate agent."

Her face turned red at the sarcastic tone in his voice. Perhaps he was only teasing, yet his failure to rejoin the comment with a 'just kidding' or a chuckle led her to believe he wasn't. "I just thought perhaps you might have heard something."

"No, can't say that I have. Sorry."

"Well, all right. Have you been back at the rec center?"

"Yeah."

"I haven't been able to go like I planned. It's been too busy."

"Actually I hadn't noticed. Sorry."

Janice felt herself growing more uncomfortable. "Oh. Well, I'm sorry I disturbed you. Good-bye." She ended the call and flopped back on her bed, covering her eyes with her hands. "What's happening?" she asked herself and God. "Everyone is against me. My mother won't leave me alone. Paul is angry with me - for what, I have no idea. The girls are upset about moving. Dear God, what am I going to do?" The helplessness descended upon her until she felt too weak to rise and face another tomorrow. Yet she must face that day, no matter what. Her girls, her mother, everyone was counting on her to continue, even if she felt like giving up.

When the call ended, Paul sat back with a sigh, convicted by his sour attitude. He knew very well Jan needed help and he ought to be willing to provide it. The confusion over his attraction for her waged a fierce battle within him. He sighed and rose to his feet, pacing the bedroom still decked out in the rosy pattern that Katy once loved. Every day since the meeting at the rec center, his thoughts of Katy dwindled to be replaced by Jan. She had ignited a spark of vitality in him; a playfulness to life that he longed to experience once again. Katy had been too weak and fragile to engage in any of the activities he enjoyed. The kids were good for a time until Katy's illness replaced the fun with the reality of life and death. Jan had refreshed his soul during the short time they were together at the rec center. Her exuberance imparted hope. Since that day, he had not been able to shake his thoughts of her.

Paul walked into the living room where the boys were engaged in a game on Len's old tablet, the one Jan had given them after Len's passing. "Anyone know of some good homes for sale?" he asked carelessly. "Your Aunt Jan needs a house and quick."

Dan didn't say anything for a few moments until suddenly he came to Paul's side with the tablet in hand. "Here's a bunch." He showed him the listings on a realty website.

Paul took it and strode back to the bedroom. He shut the door and took up his phone. "Look, I'm sorry for my attitude," he said quickly when Janice answered in a calm, soothing voice that sent a chill racing through him. He fought to steady his voice, even as his legs swayed back and forth. "The boys found you some houses on this one website."

"Oh thank you, Paul. What did you find?"

He read down the list, then listened to the scratching of a pencil as Jan took notes. He imagined her long fingers with shapely nails manipulating the pencil - the same fingers that plunged through the water in the pool, and offered him a towel after the swim. She had a great figure, a face boasting a pretty smile, and shining emerald colored eyes. She possessed a kind attitude and a willingness to join in the fun that life had to offer. Her characteristics intrigued him, more than he cared to admit.

"Paul, are you still there?"

"Yes, I'm here. Well, what do you think?"

"Actually, most of these homes I've already seen. Thanks anyway."

"Oh." His heart sank.

"I appreciate you trying."

"Sure. If there's anything else I can help out with, let me know."

"I will. Good-bye."

He ended the call and sighed once more. He wondered what to do about the strange sensation swirling around inside as if their paths in life were destined to intersect somewhere in the near future.

Chapter 13

Janice wiped the sweat from her face while she packed up several last minute boxes with breakable china and glassware. On the floor of the back room, Mary and Lisa lay curled up in their sleeping bags, anticipating the move the following morning. The last few days had been busy as well as emotional. Each time Janice picked up a letter or a piece of clothing that was Len's, the reminders churned up the grief. Her mother seemed emotionless about the whole situation, even offering to take Len's possessions they had discovered in the closets over to the Salvation Army. While Janice worked, she felt she was not only cleaning up her house, but also her life--giving away memories, scrubbing away dreams. She prayed that in the days ahead, God would fill the emptiness left in its place.

As she wrapped a goblet in a tuft of newspaper, she wondered about Paul and the children. Several weeks had gone by since she even thought to check up on the family, with her days consumed by finding a house to rent, along with all the packing required. She placed the glass into the box, keeping the corner of her eye trained on the phone. Perhaps she could make a family affair out of the move. It would ease Mary and Lisa's anxieties regarding their new home if their cousin Karen was around to keep them company. She could use the burly muscles of Paul and his boys to help move the boxes that her church had graciously packed into a moving van earlier that day.

Janice wiped her hands on a paper towel and swiped up the phone, quickly dialing the number. "Hi Dan. It's Aunt Jan. I was wondering about you all."

"We're okay," answered a solemn voice.

Immediately her insides came to attention. *No, things are not okay...again. Oh God, when will You help ease the burden in that family?* "How's school?"

"Okay. We had our first basketball game last night."

"And?"

"We lost."

"Oh, I'm sorry to hear that." She thought rapidly, wondering how to elevate his mood. "Listen, I was wondering if you big guys wouldn't mind helping me out with my move in the morning. The church packed up the van, but I could use the extra hands moving the boxes into the house I'm renting. And I pay pretty good too, including pizza."

"Wow, sounds cool. I know Pat and I can help. I don't know about Dad."

"Is he at the rec center?"

"No. He's out with Evelyn. Well, I'm supposed to call her Ms. Heckard."

Evelyn? Her fingers immediately tightened around the phone. *Who in the world is Evelyn?*

"She works at school with Dad," Dan explained to her unanswered question. "We can't stand her. It's weird. First she started out by telling Dad all sorts of things he was doing wrong in the school system. Next thing we know, she and him are spendin' all this time together." He coughed uneasily. Fear laced his words. "Aunt Jan, I don't want Dad seeing her. She's divorced, you know, with three kids of her own. Maybe you can talk him out of it. You're good at telling him what needs to be done. I think he'll listen to you."

"Dan honey, I can't do that. Your father is a grown man. He has to make his own decisions."

"I don't like it that he does this without even telling Pat and me. I had to find out in school. All the kids are talking about it, how our dad and Evelyn are hanging around each other. Someone asked me if I'd like Evelyn as a mother. I nearly knocked him down."

"Dan, I'm so sorry about this. Really though, your dad has to work this out for himself."

"Pat and I can't stand this. Karen's too young to understand what's going on. She likes Evelyn anyway because she gave her a huge walking doll that her daughter didn't want anymore."

Janice began feeling faint as her mind slowly digested this news.

"I probably shouldn't be telling you all this," he continued, "but I have to. You've got to do something to stop this, Aunt Jan."

"You know there isn't anything I can do."

Disappointment filled his voice. "Yeah, well I gotta go. Pat and I will be over to help you tomorrow. But don't count on Dad."

"Thanks so much. And Dan, all you can do is pray that your father makes the right decision."

"Yeah," came the mute voice. "I've prayed a lot, Aunt Jan, but it doesn't seem like God's listening anymore."

When the call ended, Janice plunked herself on the carpeted floor and began to pray. "I know what he means," she said to herself, recalling the times she spent in earnest prayer to God for Len's recovery, only to find him taken from her. She found it difficult during those times to understand God's will in situations like this. Now on top of it all, she had to hear the news of Paul and Evelyn. To her surprise, tears gathered in the corners of her eyes. "Oh, what do I care what Paul does with his life?" she scolded herself. "He's a grown man, after all. I just didn't know he..." She paused, twisting her fingers. "I didn't know he cared about someone else."

Sleep refused to come that night. Janice tossed and turned inside her sleeping bag. Normally her mind would be consumed by thoughts of the impending move, but this night, she could only think about Dan's phone call. The stress of the move was bad enough without added turmoil thrown into the mix. For long moments she stared up into the ceiling of the empty master bedroom, picturing Paul waltzing off with another woman, sharing in laughter and a meal in a fine restaurant under the glow of candlelight. The idea of losing someone so closely bound to the memory of Len left a lump in the pit of her stomach. How could she let Paul and his family walk away? If he found another woman to marry, he would have nothing more to do with her family. They would be bound only by the fact that her two girls were his nieces, but even that might not be enough of a relation to keep them in contact. If Paul left, a living reminder of Len would be gone. Janice pressed her face into her pillow already damp with tears.

"Janice, you have to let it go," she told herself, wiping away the tears with her fingers. "Everything in your life is on the verge of massive change. You're moving away from the life you built with Len. You have to leave it all behind, including Paul, or you will be bound by this forever." The words she spoke did little to relieve the persistent ache in her soul like a tooth in need of a new filling. "That's my problem," she reasoned as a hand clutched the corner of her pillow. "I have a hole in my heart and nothing to fill it."

The next morning, Janice forced her cares aside to focus on the events surrounding the move. As promised, Pat and Dan arrived by bicycle to help place the final boxes inside the truck. Janice offered the boys the front seat of the truck while Mary and Lisa went along with their grandmother in Janice's car, bringing with them the household plants and the hanging clothes.

She patted the front seat beside her. The boys hopped in with an enthusiasm that warmed her heart. "I'm glad you could make it. I need all the help I can get."

"Dad was gone early this morning with Karen to buy her shoes or something," Dan commented. "There wasn't much else for us to do 'cept games, and I do enough of that."

Janice placed the truck in gear, glanced out the mirrors, and slowly depressed the accelerator. The companionship of the boys gave her confidence behind the wheel of the massive truck that would have otherwise sent her nerves on edge. "Here we go," she sang. The truck groaned as it slowly proceeded up the street. "At least the house we're renting isn't but a few miles away. I can't imagine driving this thing on a long distance haul."

The boys sat in silence, staring out the window. Finally Janice asked about their ill-fated basketball game.

"I made ten baskets," Dan said.

"Dad just yelled at me," Pat added, sinking his chin in his hand.

Janice cast him a look. "Why did your father yell at you?"

"He said Pat wasn't trying hard enough," Dan interjected.

Pat shook his head. "That wasn't it at all. I played fine - the coach even said so. Dad's just plain weird now that he's seein' Evelyn. He's mad about everything."

Janice raised an eyebrow in curiosity. "I thought he would be happy finding someone special to be with."

"No way," the boys hooted in a chorus.

"He's not happy," said Dan. "He tries to act like it, but I know he's not. And she's not hashtag *special.*"

"Once I found Dad staring out the window of the bedroom," Pat added. "I mean, just staring, like he was hypnotized or something. I tried talking to him, but he just ignored me, like I wasn't even there."

Janice blew out a sigh. "Boys, I know it's hard, but you're going to have to try and be supportive of your father right now. He's going through a lot of changes. I know you don't understand why he acts the way he does. He'll get over it with time. I did and I'm still cheerful. See? Grin!" Janice put on a tooth-filled grin that stretched from ear to ear, sending the boys into a round of laughter.

"You're a cool person, Aunt Jan," Pat said. "I mean, after seeing Evelyn and all, you're amazing. For one thing she's got this real high laugh, like a hyena. And she says the weirdest things, too."

"Now boys," Janice began again.

"And she can't cook nothing," Dan added. "I mean, your cooking is awesome, Aunt Jan. And you can bake, too, with all those cool cakes and everything."

A flush filled her face. When they came to a modest ranch home with a *For Rent* sign decorating the front yard, she slowly brought the truck to a halt. "Here we are. You boys work hard for me and I'll give you ten dollars each, plus a pizza party."

"Awesome!" they cried together as they scampered out, ready to begin unloading boxes. Janice smiled to herself as she pocketed her keys, then began the long task of sorting out boxes and moving them into the tiny home. After about an hour of work, it became clear that the small dwelling would not begin to accept all the items from the large home she once owned. After a time she began the painful task of separating items that would need to be sold or given away.

"What a shame," Lucinda commented, pointing to an antique chair. "This has been in the family for generations, Janice."

"I know, Mother, but there just isn't any room."

"I wish I had room at my apartment. Oh well, I suppose it can't be helped."

The hours flew by while the boys made slow, careful work of placing boxes into the various rooms. The girls skipped from room to room, their high chattering voices filling the air as they exclaimed their excitement over the new home. When the noon hour came, Janice called for the pizza and poured out sodas for the thirsty crowd.

"You boys have been a blessing," she told them, handing them each a ten dollar bill.

Each boy stared longingly at the bill in their hands, then shook their heads and surrendered the tender to her surprised hand. "We talked it over, Aunt Jan. We decided we can't take your money. You don't have anyone to help you. Dad should have been here to help, but he wasn't. So you keep it for Mary and Lisa."

"Now I promised you," Janice began, bewildered by the gesture.

"Look, there's only one thing you can do for us," Dan said with a pleading tilt to his voice. "Tell Dad to get rid of Evelyn."

Janice shook her head and sat down with the boys on the front steps. "Now look guys, I already told you that...."

"I know what you told us, but Pat and I have been talking. If Dad wants a new wife so bad, we think it should be you. After all, we should have a say as to who will be our mother, right? Dad isn't the only one who's had a loss. We have, too."

The suggestion struck Janice square in the heart like a fist. Her hand flew to her chest. Air puffed out of her in quick heaves.

"Why not?" Dan said with Pat nodding his head in agreement. "It make sense. You lost Uncle Len and we don't have a mom. You're practically a mom to us as it is. We can be a family. We're all related anyway."

Her knees knocked together which she fought hard to steady. "Now boys...," she began in a strained voice when an angry shout came from the street. The boys and Janice looked up in start to see a minivan roll by.

Paul stared out the driver's window with a face crimson from some untold rage. "What's going on here?" he shouted, pulling the van to the curb. "I've been looking all over town for you guys."

"We were helping Aunt Jan move," Dan said.

"We left a note," Pat added.

"And how am I supposed to know where you trucked off to?" He opened the van door and jumped out, followed by Karen. His brown eyes glared at Janice. "Just what do you mean by hauling my kids away?"

"I asked them to help me," Janice began, sensing an indignation rise up within her in response to his anger.

"We offered..." Dan said.

"We didn't think you'd care what we did anyway," Pat added in a tight voice.

"Well, I do care. I care that my kids could be anywhere in the state and have no idea where."

"Yeah, like you really care where we are," Pat retorted. "All you care about is your weight-lifting and hanging out with Evelyn."

Paul's tawny complexion turned purple with rage. His fists clenched. "How dare you speak to me like that." He advanced toward his eldest son with his fist raised.

"Paul, stop!" Janice cried, stepping between the warring father and son. "Don't blame the boys. I just wanted them to help me. I should have told you where the rental house was located, but you were unavailable and...."

"Unavailable my foot. You bet you should have told me what you were doing before you go dragging my kids away! Now you boys get into the van right now. You both are grounded for the week. No basketball for either of you."

"Dad you can't do that!" Dan protested, his voice choking in distress. "Our team needs us!"

"You should have thought of that before being disrespectful and disobedient to my authority. Now get into that van this minute."

The boys slowly walked to the van, scuffing their feet along the sidewalk, muttering discontent under their breath. Janice watched them with tears in her eyes. She came forward and caught Paul by the arm. "Don't do this to them, Paul. They gave their heart and soul to help me today. Aren't you proud of the fact that they were willing to help a family member? Don't punish them for being thoughtful nephews."

He jerked around. A jolt of pain crossed his eyes. He shook his head before removing her hand from his arm. "If you hadn't interfered with our lives, none of this would be happening. My kids are now in open rebellion because of you. So I would appreciate it if from now on, you leave my family alone." He whirled, ready to storm off toward the van.

"No, I won't, Paul!" Janice shouted, her extremities trembling from the accusations hurled at her. "Whether you like it or not, they're my nephews. I love them. I won't turn my back on them, or you for that matter." Paul only continued to walk away, as if caught in a daze, until he entered the driver's seat. The tires sped off with a squeal, leaving faint traces of tread marks on the road as evidence of his fury. Janice could only throw her hands into the air, wondering when this nightmare would ever cease.

For the rest of the week, Janice walked about in a fog. With mechanical motions she unpacked the boxes and arranged her home. Inwardly her joy had been stripped from her like a flowering plant yanked out of the fertile ground. Every day she fought to restore her own happiness in the situation. She participated in events within the church, sang songs to her girls, and read the Bible. If it were not for the love she felt toward her nephews and niece, she would leave Paul to wallow in his anger and disillusionment. But in her heart, she knew she could never abandon them, no matter how Paul treated her. Nor could she abandon him, for that matter.

One afternoon as she was arranging the dishes in the cupboards, the phone rang. To her surprise it was Dan, breathless as if he had just run a mile.

"Dan, are you all right?"

"Yeah, I'm okay," he sputtered. "Listen Aunt Jan, I was wondering if you want to come watch a basketball game at the gym tonight?"

"I'd love to! What time is it at?"

"I told him eight, I mean the game's at eight. Can you make it?"

"Of course I can make it to see my famous nephews play!"

"Awesome. Thanks."

The invitation sparked a bit of happiness within her until she thought of Paul. What if he was there and still harboring anger from their recent confrontations? She shook her head, dismissing the thought. The boys had invited her, and she would attend, no matter what transpired.

Janice arrived at the Middleview gymnasium to hear a lone basketball bouncing along the smooth wooden floors. A swish alerted her to the sound of the ball neatly slicing through a basket with little effort. She smiled to herself in anticipation, patting her cell phone in her pocket. She planned to take some good shots of the game. When she entered the gym, she stopped short in a start. The bleachers stood empty of cheering crowds urging on the team. No uniformed players lined the court. A lone figure stood in the middle of the free throw circle, tossing two handed shots into the basket. From the height and muscle mass of the player, she knew it was not a high school student. Her eyebrows drew together in confusion. With tentative steps she approached the player who raised the ball in the air for another shot.

"Excuse me, but can you tell me where the game will be tonight?"

The player whirled about. All at once she found herself face to face with Paul. Sweat dribbled down his face, staining his T-shirt as he tossed the ball into the air. "What are you doing here, Jan? There's no game tonight."

"But there has to be. Dan called and told me to come watch the game tonight."

Paul shook his head, his lips forming a tight smirk. "Sorry. The boys are coming here to play a little game with me." He glanced at his watch. "And they happen to be late."

"That's funny. I thought they wanted me to watch one of their regular games. I guess they meant for me to watch a practice instead." Paul shrugged away her confusion and returned to his game. Janice took a seat on the bleachers to mull over the situation. He continued to pitch the ball toward the basket in a series of throws while Janice sat and watched. The ball hit the backboard numerous times before bouncing into his arms. Again he tossed the ball, this time sailing it cleanly through the basket.

"Two points," she shouted with a smile.

Paul flashed her a grin and dribbled the ball across the shiny, waxed surface of the court. "Want to see me make three?"

"Sure. You do it and I'll take your picture and have it put on the front page of the sports section."

"You're on." Paul positioned himself beyond the free-throw circle, pointed the ball at the basket, and with a heave, performed a jump shot in the direction of the basket. The ball spun around like a top until it fell through the basket. Janice jumped to her feet and snapped a picture.

"Score!" he shouted. "Three points. If only my boys were here to see this. Of course they aren't. They won't believe I did it."

"Yes, they will. I got a great shot." Janice waved her cell phone. "It will look excellent in full color."

"Sure, with a dripping T-shirt and hair like I emerged out of a twister."

"Since when have you been so concerned about your appearance?"

Paul took a moment to swipe down the locks of hair standing at attention from the exercise. He then took the ball in one hand, marched over to the bleacher, and posed with a foot resting on the bench. "Okay, try this."

Janice took another shot. "Perfect. Just right to email to *Sports Illustrated*." Her grin melted away as he stared at her with an expression she could not decipher. She quickly diverted her attention to the screen on the phone.

"How about playing a little game of one on one while we wait for the boys?" Paul offered, twirling the ball around in his fingers.

"Who, me?"

"Sure. You're athletic, aren't you? At least you gave the impression of a world class athlete at the rec center a month ago."

"All right. I'm glad I wore my sneakers. Just tell me what to do."

"You guard me with what's called man on man defense and try to prevent me from making a basket. You guard like this." Paul extended his arms. "Just don't trip me up or you'll commit a foul. Then I get a free throw."

"I'll do my best." Janice took her position with her arms extended as he had demonstrated. He began to dribble while she hopped back, retreating further and further until he positioned himself for a lay-up shot and made a basket.

"Oh, no fair!"

"You'll get the hang of it. Now it's your turn. Can you dribble the ball?"

"I don't know. I'll give it a try." Janice began to dribble while Paul guarded her. She advanced tentatively at first, then yanked the ball up for a jump shot, making the basket.

His eyebrows lifted in amazement. "Whoa, nice shot. Where'd you learn to do that?"

"Uh...I played a little basketball in high school."

Paul crossed his arms before his chest. "Really now. Just how good were you?"

Janice began to dribble again, moving from side to side as Paul found himself hurriedly retreating from her aggressive play. She flung the ball upward in a hook shot, scoring a basket.

"Four to two," she breathed in delight.

"Okay, my turn," he said in a guarded voice, yet with a twinkle of admiration in his eye. He dribbled down one side of the court to the other, then raised the ball to shoot a basket. Janice lifted her hand and batted the ball away.

"Hey!" he cried, racing after her. She made a fast break down the court, dribbling the ball to the far side of the gym, and up into a lay-up for a basket that just missed its mark. Paul raced and caught it on the rebound. He headed back for his own basket as Janice guarded his advance. During the dribble, she again thrust out her hand and stole the ball.

"What are you doing?" he cried, once more racing after her while she dribbled madly to the other end, making the score six to two. "What do you mean you don't know anything about basketball? You've stolen the ball from me twice!"

"I did leave out one small detail," Janice confessed with a smile. "I was the number one stealer on my team. Even made All American."

"So the truth comes out." This time he dribbled as fast as he could, managing to outmaneuver her for a basket. Both were sweating profusely when they paused to catch their breath.

"Okay," Janice puffed, praying for the energy to continue. The muscles in her legs began seizing in protest of the vigorous exercise. She dribbled slowly at first, watching Paul's advance. His hand came out to knock the ball away. She switched the ball to the other hand and began dribbling once again.

"You're ambidextrous, too?" he sputtered. "I don't believe my luck." Suddenly he lurched in front of her and the two fell into a heap on the floor. The ball rolled away out of reach. Paul scrambled to retrieve it. Janice yanked on his arm.

"Hey!" he protested. "You're obstructing my advance! That's a foul. I get a free throw."

She laughed as they both lunged for the ball. Instead they found themselves wrapped in each other's arms on the floor. His sweaty face brushed hers. Breath that smelled of peppermint gum fanned her face. Lips pressed tenderly against her cheek. Arms curled around her in a warm embrace. She thought of pulling away, but found herself melting in the kisses that drifted across her cheek and to her lips, filling her parched being with tenderness and warmth.

Paul suddenly pulled back, staring at her wide-eyed as if shocked by what had occurred. "I don't believe I just did that."

"It's all right," she said softly.

"No, it isn't. I shouldn't have done that. I don't know what got into me." He swiped up the ball, took to his feet, and began marching to the exit.

"Paul, wait! Why are you running away?"

He froze in his tracks. "I'm not running away."

"You're not?"

She watched his head sink to his chest as he fiddled with the basketball in his hands. "Okay, I guess I am."

Janice approached the forlorn figure. She reached out her hand and rested it on his forearm. His hand cupped hers with a slight squeeze that sent reassurance flowing through her.

"I run from everything," he repeated. "I've been running for so long, I don't even know when I'm doing it." He turned, fixing his eyes on hers. "But I know for a fact that I've been running away from you. I don't know what it is, Jan, but there's something very special about you. Ever since that day at the pool, I can't stop thinking about you. I've tried to let it go, but I can't. The more I try, the more angry and frustrated I become."

"Then maybe you shouldn't fight it," she whispered. "Maybe you need to let go of it and let God take care of this."

"Let God take care of it," his voice echoed in scorn. "That's a new one. I haven't let God do anything for over a year. Dan's the true Christian of the family. I don't even lead in that area anymore. I know I need to find a new life after Katy, but I avoid the change like the plague. I want to be strong and crazy to keep the kids sane, but they're going insane, and me with them."

"Paul, I know what that feels like. I really do. I was there. I felt like I was going crazy. Once I let God back in my life, He helped restore order to all the chaos. When I found Him, then I could find the new life He had planned for me."

Paul nodded in agreement, and without the challenge she had expected. Janice inhaled a sharp breath, thankful for the change, no matter how small. Now she watched him spin around and stare at the empty gym. "I just realized something. Those boys of mine never did show up for our practice."

Janice glanced around when a thought came to mind. "Maybe they planned it that way."

"What do you mean?"

"Paul, the boys care about you so much. They think I might be able to help you. They probably wanted to give us time together. I'm sure of it."

"Those kids," he muttered, bouncing the ball on the floor. "Anyway, I'm glad they did. I had fun, more than I care to admit."

Janice smiled. "So did I."

Chapter 14

Janice felt like she was walking on a cloud. Something wondrous had occurred during that time with Paul on the basketball court. A day did not pass by when she didn't think of him. At times she would sit on the couch with her cell phone in hand, waiting for a text message or hoping it would ring and hear his soothing voice in her ear, talking about his day. He called once since the basketball game, inviting her and the family out for pizza. During dinner, Janice sensed his eyes staring at her, even as she tried to concentrate on eating her pizza or pouring out more soda from a plastic pitcher for her daughters. The boys soon left to play video games, pulling Mary and Lisa along in such a way that raised both suspicion and eyebrows. Janice found herself alone with Paul in the booth. He made some comment about the pizza and how he used to love anchovies. Then he attempted to talk about that evening on the basketball court.

"I don't really know what to say," he finally admitted after trying to relay his thoughts that came out in a jumbled mass of ideas. "I guess I'm not sure about us. You remember what Len accused us of back when he was alive...and now look what's happened."

"Paul, none of it was true at the time. Our lives are so much different now. You can't compare this to back then."

"I know. I guess it's hard for me to let go and think that we could go on with life with our spouses gone. I feel like I should hold myself back for Katy's sake. I made a commitment to her."

"Until death do you part," Janice said. "As hard as it is, we don't have Len or Katy anymore. My mother was right. She told me after Len's funeral that I had to learn to live again. Don't try and relive the past. Think about the future, for the kids and for us. Let life begin again."

The words had affected him, for his facial muscles softened. He nodded his head before picking up a glass of coke and emptying it. Janice watched him drink, admiring the taunt muscles of his arms from his efforts in weight lifting, and the strong hand that held the glass to his full lips. When he finished, she dropped her gaze back to the slice of cold pizza decorating her plate. A flush crept into her face, realizing how attractive he was to her.

"I know things aren't the same," he said. "I guess we should let God take it from here and see where it leads us."

Suddenly the phone rang, jarring Janice out of her thoughts. The voice was calm, deep, and steady, just as she had imagined. She felt a tingle race through her. Could she be falling in love with him?

"So how about it?"

"What?"

His laughter filled her with joy. "You didn't hear a word I said, did you? Are Mary and Lisa acting up?"

"Oh no...I'm just thinking."

"Anyway, do you want to go ice skating with me at that new indoor rink? It's about an hour's drive from here. The kids and I went a few weeks ago and it was great. Of course, I couldn't help but remember you and I out there on the ice. Boys are fine, but you can't very well skate pairs with them. And Karen needs a little more work."

"I suppose."

"So what do you say?"

Janice reflected on that ice skating occasion long ago with his family. Though she dare not contemplate the moments spent with Paul while Len was alive, she now reflected on the way they slid across the ice, and the feel of his hands in hers, guiding her along.

"Yes, I'd love to go."

"Great! I'd take you Saturday, but I have something I'm involved with. How does Friday night sound?"

"Sounds great. See you then." Janice put down the phone and sighed, feeling like a young girl again with butterflies flitting in her stomach. She imagined then what she would wear to such an event. Did she dare try to outfit herself in tights and a little skirt? Perhaps a big sweater and a scarf looped around her neck, along with black earmuffs to match. She giggled at the thought of her dressed as some young girl, trying to impress a boyfriend. No, she would just be herself for this date.

Janice inhaled a sharp breath. A date. She was actually going out on a date with Paul. It seemed too unbelievable to imagine. A real date, and with a man who so reminded her of Len that it unnerved her at times. She had to keep reminding herself that Paul was not Len. Even if they were brothers and held to similar characteristics, Paul had his own way of doing things. He was much more carefree with life. Len had always been serious, never in the mood to play or act up. Paul liked to act young. It kept him young in many ways.

For several days leading up to the big night, Janice tried to imagine what would happen. How would she feel with Paul's hand in hers leading her around the ice, feeling the tickle of his warm breath caress her ear as he sang his favorite song? She could see him twirling her around, his laughter filling her with joy. They would go to the concession booth for mugs of hot chocolate decorated with whipped cream and find a cozy booth to sip their drinks and talk about their lives. When the evening was over, they would walk back to car, giggling about their times on the ice. She would sit quietly in her seat, anticipating what would happen next. A dark street with just the moon shining overhead to give them a bit of light...his arms curled around her for comfort...his lips full and moist on hers....

Her pulse raced at the thought. Was it wrong to think about such things, knowing she once had a relationship with Len? Janice reached over for a photo of her and Len, taken on one of their trips to the tropics. He appeared bronzed and handsome in the photo, with a huge smile decorating his face. "Len, what would you say if I told you that Paul and I might be falling in love? Would you be angry with us? Would you blame us like you did when you were alive?" Janice shook her head, opened a drawer to the lamp stand, and placed the photo inside. No, she couldn't relive those memories. She had told Paul that times were different, that their lives were different, that the must go on and not allow the memories to hold them back.

Friday arrived and Janice felt more nervous than the day she and Len were married. She settled on an outfit for skating--a wool Icelandic sweater and stretch pants that could be tucked into the skates. She even found a pair of earmuffs. A young high school girl from down the street would soon arrive to watch Mary and Lisa. The two little girls were all giggles over their mother's date with Uncle Paul.

"So Mom, does this mean you love Uncle Paul?"

The comment issued by her eleven-year-old daughter sent Janice whirling around as she stood at the counter, scrubbing it clean with a sponge in an effort to calm her anxiety. "Mary! Why do you say that?"

"Karen told me on the phone when she called the other night that Uncle Paul likes you a lot. In fact," Mary leaned her head close, her eyes widening in anticipation, "she says he loves you."

"Oh, now stop it," Janice murmured. Her fingers squeezed out the water to the sponge. Was it that obvious to the kids?

"The other night when they were here for dinner, I saw Uncle Paul put his arms around you and give you a hug. That means he loves you, doesn't it?"

Janice felt her face burn. And to think she was embarrassed by the perception of an eleven-year-old. "He was just being nice, Mary. After all, we are related."

"I think it's way more than that," the young girl noted before skipping off to play with her sister, Lisa.

Janice considered the comment while she finished cleaning the kitchen. If the children could detect love in the air, then it must be true. Time crawled by for Janice while she awaited Paul's arrival. The babysitter came and entertained the girls in their bedroom, playing with the assortment of Barbie toys they had acquired over the years. She checked the window for the small car Katy once used to drive back and forth from work. It seemed hard to believe how much their lives had changed. She hoped and prayed she was doing the right thing. Ten minutes passed, then twenty. *Where is he?* Fear entered her heart at the thought of him in a car accident. When a half-hour passed, Janice called the home just to make sure the plans hadn't changed.

"Hi Aunt Janice," Dan greeted.

"Is your father there?"

"No."

"Then he must be on his way here. I hope the car didn't break down or something." Jan detected whispers in the background until Dan's voice came over the line.

"Did Dad call to tell you?"

"Tell me what?"

"Uh...well..." Dan paused. "He hasn't been home at all yet. He's still at school."

"At school?" Janice furrowed her forehead. "Why?"

Again there was a hesitation, as if her nephew struggled to tell her the truth. When he finally explained that Dad had been staying after school, working with Evelyn, Janice blew out hard sigh. "I see. Exactly what does your father and Evelyn do?" She paused. "Never mind, you don't need to answer that. It's not your fault."

"I'm sorry, Aunt Jan. I'll tell him you called."

"No, that's all right. Thanks." Janice ended the call, numbed by the events that had transpired. All week she had been floating on a cloud that had propelled her to the wonderful land of love, only to find out that Paul was involved with someone else. "I guess I was getting mixed signals," she noted glumly, calling for the babysitter and informing her that she could go home. When Mary and Lisa found out that the date had been canceled, they looked at each other in surprise.

"There has to be a reason, Mom," Mary stated emphatically. "Uncle Paul probably had to work late."

"Oh there's a reason, all right. It's just not the kind of reason I want to think about right now." The rest of the evening she sat on the couch and moped. At times she thought of picking up the phone to call him and ask about the broken engagement. She decided this was his doing and he should be the one to make amends.

Suddenly the phone jarred her out of her thoughts. She picked it up to find his soothing voice in her ear.

"Jan, I am so sorry about tonight. I wanted to go but..."

"I guess you had to work late."

"I got caught in the middle of something and couldn't get out of it. I hope the boys called to let you know."

"We talked," Janice said, not willing to get her young nephews in trouble for forgetting to call. Despite his apologetic voice, she couldn't get the other woman out of her mind. He asked if they could have coffee over the weekend, which she reluctantly agreed to. After she hung up the phone, she sat on the couch, more confused than ever over the direction of their relationship. Perhaps Paul just needed a friendly face to talk about his life. Maybe God did not mean for them to have a serious relationship other than that of relatives who conversed about the happenings in their lives. "Whatever you want, God," she said resignedly. "Just please, don't set me up for another fall in my life. I can't lose my heart to two men, and men who are brothers."

Chapter 15

Janice slid the meatloaf into the oven where russet potatoes sat aligned in a row. The dining room table was set for seven, with tall glasses on the ends for the grownups and smaller glasses on either side for the kids. This was the second time this week that Janice invited Paul and the kids over for dinner. On the counter sat the cake she had fashioned into a snowman, with coconut sprinkled over the mounds of white frosting. The weeks had flown by and already the holidays were descending upon her. When she glanced up at the calendar to find it the first of December, her heart raced with the plans that must be made. In the midst of it all were the growing feelings she had for Paul. They met regularly at the coffee shop where Paul reminisced about his childhood with Len, and his days in college. She never realized his athletic abilities in his younger days - including playing defensive corner in football and participating in the long distances in track. She asked with a laugh why he had never chosen basketball after their impromptu game of a month ago.

He smiled with a radiance that nearly took her breath away. "Len and I always used to play at the basket Dad set up for us. But I never joined the team." He stirred cream into his coffee. "It's a funny thing."

Many times Janice thought to mention Evelyn to him, but never found the courage to bring up the subject. He seemed willing to spend time with her as friends, so she let it go until a more appropriate time. One day she would have to ask him. Each time they came together for conversation, she felt herself swept away by his charm. Yet the other woman remained in the back of her mind like a nagging ache that never found relief. If only she could know the truth once and for all.

The door to her small rental home burst open, admitting an array of cheerful faces. Mary and Lisa raced out to meet their cousins. Janice stooped at the oven to check on dinner, when a muscular arm encircled her, presenting a bouquet of pink carnations before her face. The contact jarred her for a moment, as did the scent of cologne drifting into her nose.

"Oh, they're beautiful!" She sighed and turned to see Paul's sparkling eyes that regarded her for several moments. "I haven't received flowers since..." She paused, deciding not to bring up a memory of Len. "Thank you."

"I remember the flowers you had on the dinner table at the other house," he commented, watching her every move as she fished out a vase from the cupboard and filled it with water. "I thought these would brighten up the table."

"They will."

He raised his head, sniffing the aroma of the kitchen. "Smells mighty good in here. Bet it's one of my favorite dishes. Roast coon."

"Dad!" Dan protested as he took a seat at the kitchen nook. A smile lay plastered on his youthful face with an expression similar to his father's.

Paul flashed his son a grin. "Did I say something wrong?"

"You know it's meatloaf."

"I should say it is," Janice added, biting her lip to stifle a giggle. It was just like Paul to lift her mood with some witty comment. "Roast coon indeed."

"And look at that cool cake Aunt Jan made," Dan pointed out. "She does the coolest stuff, doesn't she Dad?"

"A snowman *is* pretty cool. In fact, they're downright cold if I'm not mistaken."

Everyone laughed. Janice marveled at the changes within the family unit compared to a few months ago - the warm laughter, the jokes, the ease with which everyone participated in communication. She wondered if the transformation was in any way related to the relationship that had built between her and Paul. *God, is this a sign of something in store for Paul and I? Or should I stop looking for signs and just be thankful for what is happening among our families?*

Dinner was a pleasant affair. The kids and Paul laughed as they shared stories about their lives. Janice had not witnessed such comfort or unity within the family since the terrible moment when their loved ones were taken away. Afterwards, the kids gathered on the carpet to play a few games while Paul assisted with the dishes.

"That was a great dinner, Jan," he said, swiftly wiping each dish she washed. "The kids are getting pretty tired of my old standbys, like fish sticks and tator tots."

"I do like to cook," she confessed. "I bake all evening at the bakery, you know, but it's nice to cook up something different besides cakes."

"Hey I was wondering if you would still be interested in going ice skating with me. I know we missed out on it a few weeks back, but I'd like to make up for lost time."

Janice froze with her hands still immersed in the dishwater. "Paul, I..."

"It'll be fun. How about it?"

Janice opened her mouth to agree, then suddenly clamped her lips shut and shook her head. "I can't Paul."

He stared. The towel nearly slipped from his fingers onto the linoleum before he caught it. "What? How come? I thought you'd jump at the chance."

"It's just that I have too many things to do around here. Christmas is coming, there's cards to write up, baking, and...."

"Jan, c'mon. There's plenty of time for that."

She dunked the dishes in the soapy water when a warm hand rested on her arm.

"Jan, have I done something wrong? Are you still mad that I had to cancel that last time? I want to make it up to you. We'll skate all day if you want."

She shook her head. "Look, I know we've had some nice talks and all, but..."

"You *are* mad, aren't you?"

"I'm not mad, Paul. You're very sweet, but there's more to a relationship than just playing sports and acting rowdy." She inhaled a breath as memories of his activities with Evelyn danced in her mind. "I don't want to be just a playmate."

Silence prevailed in the room. Out of the corner of her eye, she watched Paul take a seat in the kitchen. A tawny hand cupped his chin. He sat thinking until he asked in a soft voice, "What do you want, then?"

Janice shrugged. Tears began to sting her eyes. If he didn't know, then perhaps she had been fooling herself all this time. Perhaps he only did think of her as a playmate while he considered Evelyn somebody worthy of his attention.

"I won't run this time, even though my feet are ready to take off. I won't leave until this is settled."

"We can't settle anything in front of the kids," Janice said.

"Dan and Pat are here. They can watch the girls while we take a walk." Paul rose and informed the kids that they would be taking a walk before heading for the closet to retrieve the coats. Janice avoided the confusion in his dark eyes as he held open the coat for her to shrug on. Outside, a pang of cold air nipped her cheeks. Winter was definitely on the way. They strode down the sidewalk together, each face focused on the pavement before them. Silvery rays of moonlight filtered through the bare branches of the trees.

"Okay, so what's up?" Paul asked.

"I don't know. I guess I feel uncomfortable, knowing there's someone else in the picture. I feel like I'm only good to play with or to talk to, like I was the kid next door."

"What do you mean someone else? Who?"

Janice began feeling hot inside her coat. "You know. That teacher from school."

"What are you talking about?"

Janice felt a vexation rise up within her. "Paul, I'm not stupid. The boys told me about you and Evelyn. I just wished you would have let me know."

"Evelyn!" Loud laughter bit the air. "Exactly what, pray tell, did they tell you about Evelyn?"

"That you and her have been going out after school. That's why you canceled our skating trip."

"Didn't they tell you the reason?"

Jan turned away, already embarrassed by the conversation. She did not want to be in competition with this Evelyn, but felt the jealousy rise up within her.

Paul sensed it too. "Jan, this is not what you think at all. Evelyn and I happen to teach the same grade of English. She was getting on my case for not teaching the kids more about the arts. I told her that's what Art Class is for. We clashed horns, then I had to compromise. We've been meeting in order to structure a drama program this winter. She knows all about plays. I'm a dunce in the area, so I've been taking lessons. Unfortunately, the night we were supposed to go skating, she had a major crisis with several kids coming down with colds, and she needed replacement actors for a play." He paused, his eyebrows narrowing before he added, "I'm not engaged in secret meetings with another woman. It's strictly school business. Period."

Janice felt herself shrink under his baneful stare. *Uh oh, I've really blown it.*

"I can't believe the kids said that Evelyn and I were going out," he grumbled. "That's the most outlandish thing I've ever heard."

"You should have told them what you were doing."

"I didn't think it was any big deal. Besides, it was business. That's what I told them."

"Paul, you drove the boys crazy! Pat and Dan were so upset about these secret rendezvous of yours, they came to me on the day of the move and asked me to help them get rid of her. They honestly thought you were wife hunting."

Paul's face turned scarlet. "Can you imagine me with Evelyn?"

"I don't know, Paul. Can you?"

"Of course not. She laughs like a hyena."

Janice continued to stroll down the sidewalk when she felt a warm hand slip into the pocket of her coat. She tried to draw away, but his fingers curled possessively around her own. "Paul..." she began.

"Jan, I know I've been selfish wanting things done my own way. I guess I have been treating you like my special playmate. But that doesn't have to be a bad thing, you know. I think athletics are a great way to find out more about a person. I know we're related because you married Len, but honestly, I know nothing about you as a person. For instance, I had no idea you were an Olympic swimmer or a star basketball player."

Janice could not help but chuckle.

"You have so many talents. I want to discover everything about you." He turned to face her; his arms curling around her. "Len was lucky to have you."

She faltered, "And...and Katy was lucky, too."

"I don't know about that."

"I know. She loved you deeply. You two were one of a kind."

"Maybe, but that kind has passed on to a better place. It took me a long time to come to grips with what Katy shared those last few days of her life. But I know she was right. She is in a better place."

The arms around her tightened, drawing Janice into his embrace. She inhaled his manly fragrance, enhanced by the cologne he wore. How she dreamed of having the arms of a man hold her close. The mere thought that those arms would one day belong to Len's flesh and blood left her shaking her head in wonderment.

"What is it?" Paul asked.

"I was thinking how wonderful God is to have knit us together like this. I never would have dreamed our lives would turn out this way."

"It is strange," he agreed. "We have always been family, but now we've taken a different turn in the road of life." He tipped up her chin, staring a moment or two into her eyes. A finger gently traced the curve of her cheek before settling it on her lips. His own lips followed. The kiss strengthened. When they parted, a mist of love swept his eyes.

"It's hard to believe that you were under my nose all this time," he marveled as they headed back for the house. "God has good plans for the both of us...to give us a future and a hope."

"He's amazing," Janice agreed. "He knows how to fill the emptiness in our lives far better than we can. And to think, the kids knew before we did."

"Huh?"

"Dan and Pat came right out and asked me to be their mother. They were so afraid you were going to waltz away with Evelyn that they wanted me permanently in the picture."

Paul's mouth fell open before replacing his astonishment with a wide grin. "Those crazy, smart kids. I've really taken them for granted. I didn't realize how much they care."

"They do. And I care, too."

"I know you do." Again the arms came forth, imparting gentle warmth. The embrace confirmed the thoughts radiating inside both their hearts...that love had come forth, despite the painful losses they had both endured.

Epilogue

"Here's the Yule log," Janice announced with delight, producing the log to place in the tiny fireplace of the living room inside Paul's home.

Everyone smiled, but Paul's grin proved the widest as he took the log from her arms and placed it on the fire. In response, the flames grew brighter, filling the room with gentle warmth on a frosty Christmas Eve night.

"So what should we do?" the cousins all asked. "Play a game?"

"I have a game we can play," Paul said, taking a seat on the couch. The girls climbed up into his lap and tugged on his shirt.

"What game, Dad?" asked his daughter Karen.

"Yeah, what game, Uncle Paul?" inquired Lisa and Mary.

"It's a seek and find game," he told them. "I'll tell you if you're hot or cold as you search for a special surprise I have hidden somewhere in the house."

The girls jumped to their feet, eager to participate.

"Go on, boys, join in."

"Aw, we'd find it right away," Dan said. "Let the girls find it."

"All right then, girls. Go for it."

Janice watched in amusement while Paul attempted to guide the girls in the direction of the mystery he had planted in the home. They looked beneath the Christmas tree standing in the corner. When he exclaimed, "You girls are ice cold!" they scampered off to the dining room.

"You're getting a little warmer," he said with a laugh.

The comment sent the girls in a flurry of activity, searching every nook and cranny of the dining room.

"What are we looking for, Uncle Paul?" Mary asked.

"You'll know when you find it. Keep searching."

The girls entered the kitchen area. When Paul informed them they were getting hotter, they opened up silverware drawers and then the cupboards to sift through the pots and pans.

"You're red hot now!"

"I found something!" Mary squealed, producing a small gift bag from inside a cake tin.

"Don't look inside the bag now," Paul instructed her. "Give it to your mother."

"It's for me?" Janice exclaimed in astonishment. Mary handed her the prize of a gift bag, decorated in holly and berry, and filled with red tissue paper. She opened the bag, peered inside, and gasped.

"What is it?" the kids cried as they pressed in close to see.

"It's...it's," she stammered, withdrawing a velvet-covered box.

"Dad, you didn't!" Dan laughed with glee, poking his father in the arm.

"What's going on?" Mary, Lisa, and Karen exclaimed at once.

Fingers trembled as Janice slowly opened the box to reveal a tear-shaped diamond in a gold setting. "Oh, Paul," she whispered, breaking out in tears that drifted down her cheeks. For the first time in years, the tears were not shed in grief or in confusion, but for a happiness she never thought she would experience again.

"We're all going to be related," Dan told the confused trio of girls. "Our mom and dad are getting married!"

The house broke into shouts of exultation. Paul took the ring and slid it on Janice's finger before bestowing a kiss.

"We have a family again," they all exclaimed to the sound of the log crackling in the fireplace.

"And we'll have new lives to cherish for as long as God gives us," Janice and Paul whispered to each other, holding hands with the children circled around them, grateful to God for life and for love.

The End

You can find ALL our books up at Amazon at:

https://www.amazon.com/shop/writers_exchange

or on our website at:

http://www.writers-exchange.com

All our romances:

http://www.writers-exchange.com/category/genres/romance/

About the Author

Lauralee Bliss is a published author of over twenty Christian romance novels and novellas in both historical and contemporary with nearly 600,000 sold. Lauralee enjoys writing books that are reminiscent of a roller coaster ride for the reader. Her desire is that readers will come away with both an entertaining story and a lesson that ministers to the heart.

Lauralee is also an avid adventurer, having hiked the entire Appalachian Trail twice from Georgia to Maine and from Maine to Georgia, one of only 24 women to accomplish this feat. Besides hiking Lauralee enjoys traveling and gardening. She makes her home in Virginia in the foothills of the Blue Ridge Mountains.

Lauralee's author page at Writers Exchange:

http://www.writers-exchange.com/lauralee-bliss/

If you enjoyed this author's book, then please place a review up at the site of purchase, and any social media sites you frequent!